THE WAR IN HEAVEN

March 97 /Toronto

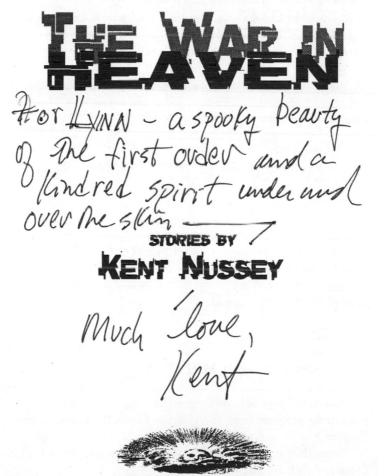

THE WAR IN HEAVEN

For Lynn — a spooky beauty
of the first order, and a
kindred spirit under and
over the skin ⟶

STORIES BY
KENT NUSSEY

Much love,
Kent

INSOMNIAC PRESS

Edited by Michael Holmes/ a misFit book
Copy edited by Lloyd Davis, Jennifer Hutchison & Liz Thorpe
Designed by Mike O'Connor
Interior photos by Michael Holmes & Mike O'Connor

"A Night in Tunisia" first appeared in *Quarry Magazine*.

Canadian Cataloguing in Publication Data

Nussey, Kent, 1954-
    The War in Heaven

ISBN 1-895837-42-1

I. Title.
PS8577.U86W3   1997   C813'.54 C96-932450-2
PR9199.3.N87W3   1997

Printed and bound in Canada

Insomniac Press
378 Delaware Ave.
Toronto, Ontario, Canada, M6H 2T8

  Insomniac Press acknowledges the support received for its
publishing program from the Canada Council's Project Grant
Program.
  The author gratefully acknowledges the support of The
Ontario Arts Council.

Thanks to Mary Cameron, Steven Heighton, Jason Heroux, Chris Miner, Barry Munger and Alexander Scala. Special thanks to Michael Holmes.

"The Weather Channel" is for Mark Sinnett and Jane Lafarga.

CONTENTS

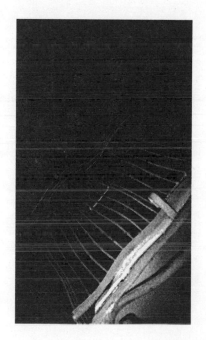

FLAMINGO: PART ONE

We're driving in the country, pushing the old Dodge just a little faster than it wants to run, just Rosemary and me, the sun and the wind and the music on the radio. The banked curves take the acceleration and throw us out the other end like a sling, so that Rosemary cries with delight, "Easy there, Mario!"

I like driving with her because Rose likes speed. Unapologetically, she loves power and acceleration, and although this car is hardly a performance vehicle, for Rosemary any ride away from town is a treat, an adrenaline holiday from her kids and her high-rise suburban hideout and the horrors that hit her as she crosses the vast parking lot between her building and the mall.

She says, "It's that point where the world falls away. You know, I must be one of the few people who loves going down the runway in a plane. It gets me excited. I mean, physically it turns me on."

I nod and say, "Escape velocity."

"That's it. Escape velocity."

She turns up the radio and puts on her 50's Riviera-style sunglasses. For the last half-hour she's been naming the songs that flow out of the speaker like bright flags snapping in the wind. There's hardly one she doesn't know. Especially corn-ball pre-rock and roll stuff. On hearing the first three notes she can name a hit by Frankie Laine or Julie London and reel off the chorus, word perfect. Driving by fields and escarp-ments and farmhouses she's been singing "What A Difference A Day Makes", "Blame It On The Bossa Nova" and "My Happiness", in a lush, plangent voice that sounds just like Connie Francis.

I mention the similarity and she confesses that Connie was one of her favourites as a girl.

"That's good," I say. "I can see you as a willowy kid kicking around some impoverished Yorkshire hollow, crooning 'Where The Boys Are'. But certainly the Beatles were big by then."

"Of course. And I was a big fan. But I always liked those American torch singers. I still do."

We swing through another curve and Rose laughs her bright, musical laugh. Just as we hit the straightaway a new song comes on and she squeezes my arm.

"Oh, I love this one."

There are no words, just the tune so familiar, so redolent of all the summers of my life, of July afternoons in air-condi-tioned supermarkets, muzak and ice-cream, the stiff thrill coming off the coolers as a pretty woman picks up a Creamsicle, then laughter on the beach, even waiting for the dentist to clean my teeth. The hidden romance in every-thing.

"What is it?" I ask her, leaning toward the dash. "God, it's so familiar. I know I know it. But what's the name? What's it from?"

"It's a movie theme. Something French from the 60's. It reminds me of these two French guys who invited me to their condo in Greece when I was just sixteen..."

Her voice trails away in a light, sweet humming, and suddenly I realize I'm in a movie with Rosemary and this is where I've always wanted to be. This is the moment and this is the woman I was dreaming about and yearning toward in the music of those empty adolescent summers.

We come off the top of the hill with a slight lift and the old Dodge lands with a jolt, and again Rosemary cries, "Watch it, Mario Lanza!"

We fly down the other side, surfing the momentum.

"That's *Andretti*," I say. "Mario *Andretti*."

She laughs loudly, pleased with her mistake.

The car levels out with the music. The windows are open, the warm wind bounces the sunshine around, whipping Rosemary's greying copper hair around her shades. She's wearing a sleeveless pantsuit of wet-looking purple, an outfit that is absolutely Rose, but it's a fashion and fabric that I can't recall seeing before. She smiles and hums, and with her hand on my knee she surveys the passing countryside like a queen.

I glance at her and say, "What's that feeling of a particular happiness, and the instant you know it, the split second it clicks, it's already begun to fade? Like right now — "

She's looking at me, waiting for me to finish, but the smile falters on her lovely face, and I realize that even these words have shaved milliseconds off the happiness I was trying to name, shrinking it by dots and hairs...

The song ends and Rosemary settles back with a lush, three-noted sigh. Her familiarity with popular music from all decades still strikes me as mysterious, like the Australian twang that sometimes slips into her otherwise posh London accents. I ask her about the music, how she can know all these songs.

"I told you, my mother sang semi-professionally. She sang

in music halls as a young woman all over England." Rose pouts a little at the memory of her mother, and says, "Also, you must remember that I didn't learn to read English until I was nine. Until then, I understood the world first hand through the senses. Music was an important conveyor of information to me. Because I couldn't read I memorized the sound of things, the meaning in the sounds. Does that make sense?"

"I guess," I say. "I guess that's one explanation."

The past has been opened and her face has gone vacant, mask-like.

"Tell me again about all those celebrities you've bumped into," I say, trying to steer her back to happier paths. "Tell me about the time you met Jerry Lewis."

She beams beneath the oversized sunglasses and launches into her tale.

"It was over twenty years ago, and we were living in a hostel for the homeless, my husband and me and the baby, in London, right across the street from the train station. Which one was it? St. Pancras, I think. I can't remember... Anyhow, I was struggling to get the pram up the steps to this horrible building where we lived and I was having a real fight with it, when this man in an American raincoat separated himself from the crowd and said, 'Allow me,' and it was Jerry Lewis! He lifted the baby and carriage all the way up for me. A real gentleman. And that was such a rotten time, too. We were broke, and living with strangers."

Again her face clouds over and she seems to be pondering some key from that time, some conundrum, that might have changed her life's course.

"That's funny," I say. "I once knew a woman who knew Jerry Lewis's granddaughter in the Philippines. That must connect us somehow."

Rose brightens and recollects meeting Richard Harris in Toronto, and then, much earlier in her life, back in London, how she'd been Roger Moore's masseuse.

"They were all perfect gentlemen," she says. "They were all

sweet and decent when they didn't have to be."

Rose still believes in gentlemen. Even after all the awful things men have done to her, she still believes that chivalrous strangers are going to save the day.

We drive without speaking, the summer fields and trees flashing by. Rosemary is lost in time while I steer through space to the music that contains both elements and therefore the meaning of our connection. There's something that I should ask her, some riddle that will illuminate her identity and purpose, that will allow me to make a decision about her, but I haven't the language for it yet.

I open my mouth to speak, but suddenly she pulls a long silk indigo scarf from her bag and wraps it around her head like Princess Grace or Isadora Duncan. The midnight-blue end flutters over her exposed shoulder toward the open window. We sail through the curves and she sings softly and brightly to the music, like a woman trying to lull herself to sleep.

Some four-corner hamlet wells into view; I ease off the pedal and cut the radio. "We'd better fill it up."

The car cruises slowly through the settlement, nothing but a mom'n'pop store and no gas. Rose reads a sign that points toward a Catholic church down a sideroad.

"When the rest of my kids are grown, I'll join a convent," she says. "After everything else, it wouldn't be the hardest thing I've done."

"Maybe there's a station down there."

I signal and turn. The street gradually descends past a few weathered houses and overgrown lots. At the shady base of the hill, where the road forks sharply, we roll to a stop on the fine gravel. We're idling beneath two huge oaks that straddle the ramshackle house on Rosemary's side. From the dim recesses of the porch comes a bright twitter and cackle, like tree spirits trying to catch our attention.

"Budgerigars," says Rosemary dreamily, and I realize I've never heard that word spoken before. Sure enough, there's the old-fashioned wire cage at rest on the railing, two or three green and yellow birds inside flitting on tiny swings. On the beam above them someone's nailed a cow skull, cracked and stained.

"This isn't good," I say. "We've got to find some gas. Or else find a short cut back to the city. One or the other is a must."

"Pretty birds," she says, dreamy and low, almost sad.

We make a quick U-turn and race back to the highway, the peaceful shade trees shrinking behind us.

"I'm sure there's a county road that'll take us straight across," I say. "If we find it, we'll probably be able to make it. Otherwise, we'll need a pump."

We drive farther down the road. No sign of habitation now, and a distinct shift in topography: more pines and rock outcroppings, like the bones of extinct behemoths, where the earth has worn away. The sky is different too; the touristy sun has been surrounded by long grey clouds in strata that seem to parallel the shelves of rock that bank the country road.

Rose contemplates the land as if comparing it to the rest of the world she's ventured upon, as if to measure its character and meaning in light of a particular beach or villa or island she sees clearly but can't quite specify in time. While we drive, the settings of her life circle her like a fantastic ring, images which are equidistant from her memory's eye and each other, which contain a world of rich options and baffling human natures she has failed or refused to learn: London, England, blends into London, Ontario; one Thames bleeds murkily into the other; blocks and streets trade names and architectures, while derelicts and cab drivers cross oceans to complete peculiar dramas that float up in disparate fragments and tags. It's all there, but it comes out in Rosemary logic, and if I ask her to provide names and dates, she says, "Well, let's see, I can't tell you the year but it was before Linda was born, and after Tracy, and we had just moved..." and linear chronology is once more thwarted and the wheel of experience is given a spin. Characters click by in no apparent sequence. The husband who drugged her and sold her to his friends is followed immediately by a kindly third-form teacher; a lesser in-between lover precedes the landlord who beat her son, and each is interspersed with shining glyphs and heraldic ornaments of memory like illuminations on ancient tombs or manuscripts, little visions of a bird at sunrise or a fish on the line, and I have only inklings of how they connect, how she got from Husband A to Husband B, from continent to continent. Rosemary's story is like a hoop of cloud, and when I try to hold it like this wheel in my hands it squirts out and doubles in with no beginning or end, no motive or fruition, only the circuit that feeds the first into the last and back again...

For an instant, as I steer us through the landscape, over the rising tilts and curves, I understand that all my rides with Rosemary are one and the same, like the möbius strip of her stories. Our time and experience together form a single fabric in a neat loop that twists at the moment when reason demands continuity, and to seek it would spell derailment for us, an absolute end to our intimacy. Even now, we are driving into the dense and radiant fog of her narrative; every item she presents as fact may be no more than a colourful mist she attaches to the larger saga to lend it a literal dimension which distracts from the gaps and imprecisions and breakdowns. At this moment, beside me in the car, she might be anyone. Clearly, she could be that high-priced call girl she'd claimed she'd been back in England. "Not a streetwalker," she declared. "There's a difference." She said she worked for an avuncular Australian who kept a stable of women on London's Park Lane for the moguls of British capitalism. Later, when I pumped for more details, she laughed sharply, "Oh, I just made that up to keep you interested."

The day she denied her Park Lane career we were riding in this car and I looked at her and realized it could go either way. All or none of it might be true. Even now, as she faces that road with pride and defiance and a beautiful inwardness

I have seen in certain statues — even now, I'm thinking, "Maybe Jerry Lewis was a grateful client..." and, "That pimp would explain the Aussie in her voice." But whatever she says is true, because the moment she says it, it's true for her. And when she denies her story it's because she's revising the past constantly; not out of deceit or scheme, but with genuine hunger for the truth, which wears different faces on different days, like Rosemary, and on any day I can only know what Rosemary knows; I can only believe what Rosemary believes at the moment she believes it.

I steal another glance at the dark glasses, at the flowing scarf and the statuesque blankness of her face. There was a bridge I crossed blindfolded the first time we made love, or immediately afterward, when we sat on the bench beside her early summer garden. That was at the rented house she soon abandoned for her cramped, aerial apartment. But we were sitting on that wooden bench after hours in bed, calm and glad just to feel the sun and breathe the warming air, when a neighbour's kid materialized and said, "Mrs. Johnson, is Talbott home?" We watched him, this kid who was ten or eleven, disappear down the driveway and around the freshly green hedge. Then I turned to Rosemary: "Who's this Mrs. Johnson?" With a slight grimace, she replied, "Ask me again in three weeks." The next month, after a night of packing boxes for the move, we stood in the vacant kitchen and she showed me three different driver's licences and a dozen credit cards in the various names. Those identities, those stories and names, are here in my car, travelling beside me. Though she often says, "Don't worry, I'm Rosemary now," there must be six different women, all ages and classes, riding in this staid Dodge I inherited from my reason-loving father. As we drive through the world I'm working on a theory and a theme, a simple musical motif which is as much as anyone can say or sing about this planet, this human place, and a theory about Rosemary which goes like this: the warm, living body, the particular woman beside me, is evolving with each new name and incarnation toward a higher, finished state which blessed few attain in this lifetime. Or, the opposite: with every vanishing act, always necessary to her physical survival, her individuality is merging and melting into a faceless mainstream one might roughly equate with her apartment tower and the low, sprawling mall across the parking lot.

She leans forward and puts her fingers to the radio knob, touches it almost tenderly, then sits back, reclining her attention to the outside scenes that fly by in a dream of summer. Certain nights, after breathless hot days, Rosemary and I lie in the large bed in her small room, enveloped by worn Turkish rugs and alabaster cats, the walls crowded with prints of frescoes from Greek or Roman ruins. Upright, in the middle of this, like a gaudy vein threaded through the sacred heart, her floor lamp twines with pink feathers on a leather thong. These are all the lovely artifacts from her previous lives. Though the best, she maintains, have been stolen or sold to put food in her children's mouths. It's the ones that disappeared into neither category that she genuinely grieves, the books or jewelry that were left on the run, gobbled up in the chaos. Once or twice a month she will say, "I wish I could find my ladybird earrings. They were my very first Mother's Day gift." Ladybird earrings, she says, again and again, and nothing is sadder or more suggestive of mortal loss than the weight of those words on her lips and tongue. The ghost of those earrings infuses every icon and pagan comfort in her room and produces an effect that is both holy and bathetic, cool and cluttered; in other words, this is purely strange, juxtaposed with the four glass pyramids topping the mall across the floodlit asphalt and the flat, suburban earth that devolves around us in dumb, electrical grids while we lie on Rosemary's sacred pink bed...

"Where the hell are we?" I say, slowing a little. "What kind of place is this?"

Rosemary sits straight and serious. Somewhere back there she took off the sunglasses.

We round a tight corner and, off to our right, about fifty yards from the car, a pair of enormous winged creatures lumber into flight, their broad greasy wings slapping the humid air. They bounce once or twice on ungainly skeletal legs and lift off uncertainly, their small black heads turning slightly in our direction.

"Christ, look at that!"

I know she has seen this double apparition, but Rose keeps her eyes trained on the winding road ahead.

"God," I say, "I've never seen anything that big with wings."

The vultures levitate and a brief black shadow darkens the hood; they become a rising obstruction between us and the sun.

"Turkey buzzards, come up from the south," I say. "Best argument for global warming."

Rose looks away and says nothing. In her soul, I know, she's gauging the signs against each other, turning over the omens again and again.

We drive on, faster. The land is all strange now, bleak and stunted, paler greens under darker skies. I coast and brake on the shoulder.

"This isn't right. We should turn back."

"A shame to backtrack."

"I know, but this isn't right. We missed that road."

I lean out the window and mark the grey clouds stacking up to the north. The air is oily, alive, in dialogue with the many stagnant lakes hidden among the rock and trees that surround us.

"Besides," I say, "it smells like rain coming. Something's happening out there."

Rosemary pulls off her scarf and pushes it into her bag. The happiness that encompassed us twenty minutes ago has evaporated, leaked into the tainted atmosphere like music.

"All right, let's go back," she says.

I turn the car around and drive slowly, watching. Before we reach the town with the budgies, I spot a country road cutting away from the highway.

"That may be it," I say. "That may be the one."

Rosemary frowns. "What makes you think so?"

I swing the wheel and we bump down the smaller road, almost immediately entering a corridor of slender, reaching trees, mostly poplars and saplings. The dust rising in the rearview blots out the world behind us. The needle on the fuel gauge flickers dangerously; I can almost hear it, like a Geiger counter.

"We'll just see how this looks," I say, though I know we're running too low to afford a mistake.

After a mile or so, Rose says, "I need to stop."

"What?"

"I need to stop. I have to go."

We drive on without speaking. Finally, I slow and stop the car.

"I'll just be a minute," she says, and she gets out, shutting the door with a desperate, careless motion.

With my hand resting high on the wheel, I wait and wonder at the synchronicities of landscape and weather, the way a particular sky seems to suit the earth beneath it. Here and now, the dense interstices of thin, dark trees and decayed white trunks appear to carry the cloud-pocked firmament in a way that transforms the conception of distance between them. Instead of indicating limitless space, the sky seems to suggest an immediate tactile entity, like an old grey saucer, flush with the mottled treetops. My eye runs over the line where the two meet, the line where mystery becomes weather, the line where skin becomes air. I close my eyes and try to feel myself inside that line, riding the tension indefinitely, trying to find its rhythm, like a wave.

A crow cries and I blink, look around, letting it all come back ordinary.

"Rosemary?" I say. "Rose?"

She's nowhere in sight. I scan the woods on her side of the car, but I have no recollection of the point where she entered the forest. I saw her climb out, heard the door slam, but after that I couldn't say. I release the seatbelt, get out and lean on the car, my bare arm on the warm metal roof.

"Rosemary?" I say again.

The trees are tangled and thin, crooked like question marks and coat hangers. The silence between and behind them is vast, impenetrable. The shadows like generations of ghosts crowded and pressed into awful histories. From the interior comes a small, placid plop like a rock falling through canopies of branches, landing with a small bounce on carpets of leaves. Above this world dim thunder rolls, and my heart quickens. I stare into the distance, following the road that makes a brittle artery between the trees.

"Rose!" I call. "What the hell — "

And just like that, I know I've lost her. Whatever intimacy and knowledge that occupied the seat beside me only minutes ago is gone, departed forever into a void that takes and takes and gives back only hints and shadows. Disappeared into that line where the treetops meet the sky, that music where time invests space with inevitability. My knees go soft and I hear myself raise her name, which is not even her real name, like I'm fixing it to the air where I saw her last.

"Don't do this," I say. "Don't do it, Rose."

I'm alone and the whole of her history is in my loss: the flight from sadistic husbands, the harsh sex and heart fatigue, night trains to new cities and handsome strangers who chipped away at her youth. New numbers and new identities, the invented names overlapping, accruing texture and density like posted bills, but so many that meaning is lost — I see that now — and suddenly the needle skips and all the small vanishments blur so that even she doesn't know who she is, even Rosemary can't keep Rosemary in focus.

I cross the road and walk up and down a narrow length where the trees begin, as if I might discover an opening, a door. There's a rumble of thunder, a rush of hot wind in the trees. Ever since we met we've been driving toward this moment.

"Goddamn it, Rosemary! Don't leave me here! Don't you leave me, Rose!"

I'm standing beside the woods, stricken and small, having stopped on that exact intersection of character parallels and destiny meridians, the trapdoor sprung on the stray moment where the unlucky ones drop from view. I'm standing at that place, just to one side, a little to the left or right, when the saplings quiver. The leaves rustle and shake somewhere behind me and she steps out of the forest on the other side of the road.

"Oh, look," she remarks distantly, "I've scratched my ankle."

I stare and wait. She walks around me and gets into the car. I wait a moment longer, then I follow, ducking into the driver's side.

Soon we're moving fast toward the highway, running in front of the storm. Rosemary's neat chin and high cheekbones are raised like a totem or figurehead. Beside me, now, she has become utterly foreign.

"What? What is it?" I ask her.

She looks away and I drive faster. The windshield blisters with the first drops of rain.

THE WEATHER CHANNEL

Each day began with the dog barking in the near distance. The horizons of the morning were fractured in all directions by animal complaints and urgencies that bled the sunlight of its spectrum and silenced the birds that once scatted from the lone birch tree in the backyard. His eyes would open after an all-too-brief and restless sleep, like the sleeps of soldiers in trenches, and he would resurface nerve by nerve, sense by sense, famished for peace but already alert to the short and guttural barks of the big dog next door that rained down on his consciousness in fusillades and salvoes, a relentless barrage that he could not escape even in the shower, where the steady barking trickled through the vent shaft over his head like an intercom or radio that broadcast nothing but dog all day long.

At breakfast the noise abated and, with his coffee in hand,

still in his unfresh sweatshirt and track pants, Fred opened the only door in the house, which fronted the dog's aluminum shed five or six yards away. He stepped into the April sunshine to level a glare, a mental vibration of sheer willed hatred that might strike the dog mute or dead. The dog, huge-chested and handsome, heard the door and lifted itself on two stout legs against the wire mesh. Its eager canine visage met the slatted human eyes. The dog's curly tail fanned the fetid air of the shed. The tail stopped. The dog barked.

Gripping his mug like a pistol, Fred turned and noticed muddy cat prints like chocolate clusters on his mother's Oldsmobile in the driveway that adjoined the neighbours' unpaved strip. The cat that had left these insults was a furtive, wild-looking thing that belonged to the same people who owned the dog. Fred touched the dried mud with a finger. The dog woofed and Fred's heart misfired. Christ, the entire household was a blight, a particular curse aimed straight at Fred, as if they trained their animals to work in tandem, the shabby cat taunting the overwrought dog into frenzies. He stared at the dirt on the otherwise shining automobile. How a cat, a traditionally clean domestic, could carry that much crud on its paws was beyond him. Maybe this cat had some raccoon in it. Or pig. Maybe these neighbours had come in from the country with their own kind of feline, an unholy crossbreed that compounded the cat's perversity with the squalor of some rooting beast.

Fred looked back at the dog in its makeshift kennel. Straining against the mesh, it whined with a sound like a high, mellow yodel, a sound that tapered, then rose to a full-blown bark, then a series of barks.

Quickly, fumbling with his cup, Fred retreated to the house and shut the door. With his back to it, he heard the dog bark and bark. Heard it, Christ, he felt it, battering the foundation of his sanity. Bad enough he was living in his mother's cramped little duplex in a depressing, down-at-the-heels suburb; bad enough his mother was succumbing to a series of strokes in a nursing home downtown. But on top of everything, he'd found himself contending with belligerent hillbilly neighbours, people so uncivilized, so unschooled in the straightforward rules of getting along, that Fred found himself entertaining bitter and half-serious doubts about the family of man as a basis for civilization.

He shook his head, as if to clear it, and refilled his coffee cup in the kitchen. He ought to dress and shave and buy a paper, check the classifieds. He sat down at the table and listened to the noise next door. It would go on and on, from sun up to late afternoon, when the kid came home from school. And truth be told, the kid himself was the real bane, scarier than anything else over there. Ten or eleven, pug-faced and overweight, with his knee-length T-shirts and squarish head topped with an industrial brushcut, this kid stalked a perpetual circuit to and from the corner store and never missed an opportunity en route to trample new grass or uproot flowers or toss a Super Slurpee container on someone's lawn. When the city surveyed the street for gas lines the kid ripped a dozen orange-tipped stakes from the earth, then broke them over his knee and piled the pieces on the porch of the retired minister who lived on the corner. Beyond that, he was always smacking a ball against Fred's mother's house or forcing his piggish body through the gap in her backyard cedar hedge, breaking branches, creating a space over months that roughly outlined his shape, so there was no casually glancing back there without being reminded of the unpleasant facts.

Fred went down to the small finished basement and turned on the TV, raising the volume against the din from next door. First he checked the local station where he'd been the resident meteorologist for five years. He watched a minute of a game show and switched to the national cable weather channel. A segment on tide movements ended and a clear-faced young man appeared beside a weather map of the country. After he lost his job, friends had urged Fred to give the weather channel a shot. Word had it the channel was bad work — long hours, lousy pay, slim opportunity for advancement — and of course he'd have to relocate. But his real reticence was philosophical: they didn't do weather the way Fred did weather. Their approach was all wrong. They trivialized it to high school science. They did weather the way McDonald's did hamburgers, the way Midas did mufflers. There was no reason to believe such an outfit would show any more tolerance for his approach than his last employers.

The phone rang upstairs. Fred listened to the jangle of his mother's old rotary job and the television sound sandwiched between it and the muffled barking from next door. He closed his eyes. The phone could be the nursing home, or the real estate agent, or his brother, who owned a chain of doughnut shops in another town. Probably the realtor, a woman named Stella Smart, whom his brother had commissioned to sell this place. The first time she looked through she recognized Fred immediately. She stood at the kitchen sink and snapped her fingers.

"Fred Scaletta," she said. "The Grim Weatherman."

For a moment her curiosity seemed to transcend her professional demeanour and she looked at Fred as though he were a flash of rare weather, a waterspout or a double rainbow. After that she was more reserved, her attitude tinged with suspicion. Stella seemed to sense that he was jamming her best efforts to sell the house, simply by appearing when he was least wanted, by sleeping an extra hour in the morning or by taking an afternoon siesta, so that his prone and snoring form on the sagging couch would dampen the interest of would-be buyers or skew her sales talk. A motivated woman with a glistening silver perm, Stella tried to sneak the public through when Fred was out on errands or down at the nursing home. But with eerily accurate prescience he was able to anticipate her arrivals with hopeful strangers. Occasionally, when they encountered him clothed and kempt, she introduced him as "Mr. F. S. Scaletta, late of the

CKWS news and weather team." Other times, when he raised his haggard and uncomprehending face from the sofa, one of the house hunters would exclaim, "Hey, you're that weather kook on TV," and he would feel oddly exalted, like some forgotten starlet recognized by crones on a bus.

When the ringing stopped he went up and disconnected the telephone. He left the television on loud while he dressed to visit his mother at the home. It was a chore he performed daily, just before noon, imposing a kind of order on his life. Stepping outside, he surprised the neighbour's cat arching its back and stretching its claws on the front tire of his mother's car. The cat shot him a feral glance and vanished, its crazy soft feet skittering on the blacktop. Fred crouched and touched the rough cross-hatchings of claw marks on the whitewall.

"Goddamn it," he said to the wheel.

The dog barked a few yards away and Fred started from his crouch. Long ago — long since talking to the fat kid's ill-tempered father and after a dozen phone calls to the indifferent by-law officers — Fred had learned the futility of reacting to the people or animals next door. He knew that as soon as he shouted at the dog, the moment he bestowed a single human word upon it, a vein of something corrosive and self-destructive would open. If he let it out, just for an instant, his day would be ruined.

As he got into the car, as the dog barked and barked, he had the powerful impression that it was trying to make eye contact, trying to goad him. As he drove around the corner and away from the house he gauged the diminishment of the dog's harangue, as if he were driving out of a rainstorm that faded in the rear-view and gradually ceased to pelt the roof of his consciousness.

For the entire hour or so spent in his mother's tidy room, or the sunny lounge where her fellows squawked or snored, Fred held himself steady and cool. But he departed with rising elation, almost euphoria, like leaving church in summer; he caught himself breaking into a tuneful whistle as he hurried along the polished corridors toward the sweet spring air.

Driving home beside the river, he cast a discerning weather eye to the heavens. Despite his high spirits he felt a leaden resentment toward the human race, particularly his brother, the doughnut mogul, who rarely visited their mother but never quit trying to pry Fred out of her house. He might have seen Fred as a caretaker, a useful presence, but since their mother had given him power of attorney his brother had made it clear that he wanted Fred out. Perhaps Stella Smart had offered an opinion. At any rate, once or twice a week he phoned with ultimatums meant to shame Fred from the premises. It was undoubtedly for the best that he lived too far away to meddle personally on the scene. Yet his older brother's judgments made Fred squirm. As if owning doughnut shops carried more weight than being a weatherman. And even if Fred wasn't currently employed, his meteorological faculties were sharp, functional, always applied to the airy world like a honed edge that peeled away the apparent and pointed to the ineluctable. Once a weatherman, always a weatherman. It was a matter of vocation. And these days there was more to the weather than met the casual eye. The planet had slipped its axis, all the old laws and patterns tilted from a broken hinge. These days, weather truly mattered. It was the only news that meant anything.

His heart quickened as he rounded the corner and sighted the shed. His senses involuntarily attended. There it was. Barking as if it hadn't stopped since he'd pulled out of the driveway. Goddamn it, was there no respite? Did the wretched animal never leave off to eat or sleep? As he swung the wheel the dog reared against the mesh, upright and ears pricked, barking and barking with something like an idiot's grin on its white and black face. Fred parked between the house and the shed. As he moved from the car toward the house the dog warbled like a soprano warming up for her recital. The dog struck the gate with its front legs and burst into a rapid-fire string of barks that emptied rhythmically from its chest like a cartridge belt. Fred wavered and swayed, caught in the cross-volley that resonated between the houses. Then he lurched toward his door, laboured with the key, and nearly fell into the darkness inside.

While Fred was eating his supper the barking stopped. He was lifting the fork toward his mouth when he noticed. How long the dog had been silent, he couldn't say, but when the silence struck him, when he suddenly felt the absence of sound, his hand froze and his vision fixed on the abstract chaos of the forked pasta in front of him. He shivered and put down the fork and held himself as still as possible, hardly breathing. The silence flared and he lurched. A car door had slammed out on the street. He turned his head from side to side; then he rose slowly from the table and switched on the radio.

The sun was setting later now, in a sea of pinks and blues almost like summer, and Fred decided he'd hook up the hose for the first time that season and wash the car. Just a good rinse to get rid of those muddy paw prints. The dog was nowhere to be seen and it felt good to drag the old green hose from the laundry room and attach it to the spigot on the side of the house. He turned the tap and felt the basement pipes shudder, as if he'd released some long-dormant subterranean power. The coils jerked, the nozzle spat; a long arc of spray fell over the driveway and spattered a hubcap. With satisfaction and relief he blasted the mud spots at close range, washing the windows and panels in lazy streams that sheeted prettily down the metal and glass. It was twilight, the sun sinking in a pool of pastels just over the hedge; somewhere back there, stirred by the smell of water on the evening air, a robin chirped her little grace note. Fred took a step with the cold current leaping from his hand, splatting pleasingly on the car's hood. It took him several instants to clue to the voice that hailed him from the neighbour's house.

"Hey faggot," it said. "Hey you! Fag!"

Fred stood and listened while the water fell on the car.

"Faggot! I'm talking to you!"

The voice came from an upstairs bedroom window, behind red, white and blue blinds.

"Hey you!" it shouted. "Hey fag!"

It was the kid. Fred could make out his shape, like a fat egg squared at the top, silhouetted in the lamplight behind the slats.

"I'm talking to you, faggot."

Fred stood and let the water rattle off the car's flat surfaces. The sun was disappearing behind him, nearly gone. He and the car and the houses to his left and right were turning into shadows, melting into the dusk. He waited until the kid quit calling, then he turned off the water, dropped the hose beside the house, and went inside.

Later that night he tried phoning a woman he knew in Vancouver. Her answering machine said she was out of the country and Fred hung up before the beep. He couldn't believe that kid next door. He wanted to laugh, and yet he felt deeply, inexplicably, grieved. Certainly there were other things to think about: angry folk in the heartland making bombs in cracked bathtubs; genocide in Africa; his own mother marking time in a nursing home, humming her tunes, reading aloud from the Bible the way a schoolgirl recites nonsense rhymes, substituting banal nouns for the heavy words of reckoning. Fred admonished himself. There were still decisions to be made, circumstances he must follow to the end. He must dwell in the present. Don't give up the job hunt. Something would materialize. It always did.

On an impulse, he turned on the weather channel. Odds were good he could get on there. Most of these guys were kids, just starting out. Obviously the better part of their attentions went into their clothes and hair. Fred had angles on weather that they couldn't even imagine. But could he tone himself down? Could he suppress his eschatological eye?

Would he be satisfied mouthing the literal facts, the highs and lows, when the earth's waters and bedrock and gases were stricken and unbalanced?

Abruptly, he changed stations, cruising the dial. He watched ten minutes of a cop drama, and then bits from a couple of harrowing tabloids. It seemed that all the shows were about teenaged killers, thirteen and fourteen-year-olds in baggy pants and baseball caps, boys and girls murdering each other and the very elderly without second thoughts. That was the story everywhere, fact or fiction: blandly homicidal adolescents without a twinge of conscience.

At last the eleven o'clock news came on the local channel. Fred waited to catch the weather. Six months ago, watching his replacement would send him into a dark and abiding funk. But now she didn't leave a scratch. He could take her long, luscious gazes into the camera and her perky blonde nature for what they were — career tools. And although the substance of her predictions was harmless and accurate enough, they struck him as nothing more than journalism, a product that had little to do with language or perception or event. They functioned instead as a kind of drug to divert people from the real catastrophes impending on the winds. And even though Fred's station bosses had charged him with distorting the facts, he still believed that his daily appearances had been a service to the viewer, a dedication to higher truths. In pursuit of the atmospherics that alter human paths, he didn't just give them the present conditions, he interpreted the signs, he projected little visions of the future in rain acidity and UV levels, and the impact of both on frogs. Once, on the air, he asked his fellow citizens, "Do you get the feeling you're on LSD when you look at our river? Have you noticed an intense day-glo quality and a truly foul smell? Do you really want your kids and pets to swim in this stuff? Don't blame me, my friends, when they go blind or grow an extra limb. They don't pay me enough to warn you seriously about that."

All of this was on a tape that his friends at the station still played at parties, but the management was not pleased. They knew he meant it. After repeated warnings, and a growing degree of direness in his on-camera asides, Fred was given notice. True, ratings had never wavered, but his superiors were convinced there was no market for cosmic alarm. And of course, they were right. Fred knew as much. Nevertheless, on the night of his final broadcast he stared down the camera and declared, "We live on the exhaust end of an old truck. Time has come to realize that the air we breathe is poison. In a decade all your deals and schemes will be rendered void by the pollution in everything, the unfiltered radiation from the sun. As a professional, it is my duty to tell you these things."

Recollecting his words, Fred felt bewildered and blue. What had he hoped to accomplish with such a performance?

Tonight's report ended with the Channel Ten weather Jane smiling suggestively and batting her eyes. After the commercial she appeared at the desk with the two anchors, her big neon blonde hair flipped over one shoulder to imply nonchalance and casual style. Watching her coy glances, Fred felt the old righteousness flare up. These glossy, vitalized men and women, some years younger than Fred, were not truly attuned to the real news or weather. They used the raw events of man and nature as a ticket into broadcasting. Their feigned enthusiasm was no more than a rung up the careerist ladder. Plainly, they weren't seeing what was really happening out there.

That night, tricking himself to sleep, Fred made up new weather. Lying there, wide-eyed in the dark, he imagined new kinds of light and precipitation. New ways to describe and interpret meteorological effects no one had heretofore witnessed. There would be new names for new clouds; new reasons for fissures in the ground. A handful of real weather heads, the determined remnant, with bona fide vocations and not just careers to guide, would explain this weather from caves and dirigibles while angry orange tides inundated the suburbs. Many domestic animals would die or be eaten by their owners in desperate need. As he waded into sleep, Fred considered the weather monks of the future making human sense of the crazy heat on the tarmac, the panic raging on the information highways. Floating away in his aerial basket, he peered down at the suffering earth through a golden telescope like someone in a Victorian science fiction novel and mapped the progress of the purple smog over the country-sides. He heard himself explain why the moon had turned scarlet and the Great Lakes gone dry. Gave his best guess as to who was safe and who must hide...

The morning broke with dogs whining and barking at the edge of his dream, frantic hounds separating him from his peace, circling beyond the thin pane of his sleep, then louder and nearer as if they were closing in for the final confrontation.

He sat up with a curse, squinting in the bleak wash of light that soaked his curtains. Almost immediately the barking stopped. Fred leaned forward and listened for another five minutes, his heart beating, his head inclined. Cars passed on their way to work. A light breeze played in the tree outside his window. Later, in the kitchen, just as he tasted his first coffee of the day, the dog started again. Fred rested his head against the wall and stared at his cup. The dog kept at it, a slow, jackhammer chant of imbecility and power that missed the odd beat so when a minute passed in silence Fred caught himself in a tension of suspense, straining both away and toward the inevitable. The dog barked; Fred started and gasped despite himself. The sound fell heavy and rhythmic, an idiot machine chipping away at the fundament, pressing closer and closer to the earth's secret nerve.

He could wait no longer. Now he knew it. It was him or the dog, civility and law be damned. It was him or them. He knelt at the cabinet beneath the kitchen sink, looking for something. While his head was in the dark, chemical space he felt the sound from next door coming down on his

exposed parts; he felt it like straight paralysing poison inject-
ed into his spine, freezing his volition, shrinking his heart.
But he would fight it. This time he would prevail.

Nothing under the sink suggested an option. He foundered
up the short flight of stairs and searched the cabinet beneath
the bathroom sink. His hand fastened on a nearly empty
squirt bottle of toilet disinfectant. He stood and pried off the
top; he scanned the rack over the sink. A small rounded bottle of his mother's perfume sat beside a larger bottle of expensive aftershave a woman had given him. He emptied both
into the plastic squirt bottle and added water. He shook the
concoction and felt his heart race. He felt like a terrorist, a
mobster, an Old Testament avenger.

Just outside the door, between his mother's house and the
car, he had the sudden sensation of being set up, duped into an
elaborate trap engineered by his brother and others, but the
dog noise flayed his nerves and froze his mind. If he did not
stop the noise, stop it now, nothing would ever be good again.

From the shadow of its shelter the dog saw him coming. As
he stepped onto the patch of lawn, the shed before him
seemed to quiver from the frenzies within. Fred saw himself
storming a machine-gun nest, charging through waves of
enemy fire, the guns all trained on him, the clear target, the
literal object of their fury. He stood close enough to the mesh
to feel the dog's warm breath and spittle against his arm. He
thrust the slightly-hooked bottle through the wire and
squeezed hard. The dog jerked its head and sneezed. The bottle asthmatically refilled with air and sprayed again, drench-
ing the dog and the straw strewn about its water bowl. The
dog scrambled backward and cocked its head quizzically.
Breathing hard through his nostrils, Fred wet the straw
behind the gate with soapy dregs.

When the bottle was empty he looked around and withdrew to his driveway. Now he felt the chill April air against
the warming sun. He looked at the street expectantly. For a
second or two the silence was complete. The morning was

pure. If only this would last. If only this was his life.

The dog barked twice, like a one-two punch.

Fred stared and took a step toward it. The voice he heard repeated itself. Slowly he turned his head.

"Is everything all right?"

He blinked at the crisp orange blazer beside the car.

"Are you okay?" she asked.

It took him another moment to recognize Stella Smart.

"Sure. I'm fine," he said. He looked at the shed. The dog seemed to be listening to them. "I'm fine," he said, turning to Stella again. The morning air carried an unnatural sweetness, a taint that came and went on the shifting breeze.

"What a morning," he said.

She jiggled the keys in her hand, making a sound that reminded Fred of high school principals or cops.

"Can we talk?" she said. "Can we go inside?"

She followed him in to the kitchen, where she dropped her key-ring on the table and glanced at the dishes in the sink.

"We're not making progress, are we?" she said. "I think it's time to reconsider our approach here."

Fred tried to listen. He knew she was telling him something important. But as she spoke he felt the barking from next door start again; he felt it go through the walls of the house. He peered at a corner of the ceiling and felt the shock waves going through the place.

"Can you hear that?" he asked, interrupting her. "Can you hear that dog?"

She frowned at Fred as though he were some life-form she'd never before encountered. She regarded him as though he were the rare specimen of some nearly extinct breed she might have read about back in school but never expected to see in the flesh. Beneath her swept, silver perm, her face registered a series of shadows.

"I've got three of them at home," she said. "They're like my babies. My buddies. I guess it's a personal thing."

Fred felt the perpetual barking go through him; he could

almost see it penetrating every cohesive atom of the house.

"But you're right," Stella offered. "Bad karma with dogs... none of it helps. None of this makes the property more attractive, does it? Frankly, Mr. Scaletta, we've got to get with it here. Have you spoken with your brother lately? I know he's been trying to reach you."

Fred realized she was looking at the empty cradle of the phone on the wall, following the stretchy cord to the receiver that lay on the table like a fish waiting to be cleaned for lunch.

She shook her head. "This is not right. This isn't the way to do things. I can't guarantee results if we keep doing it this way. You've got to realize," she said, and she looked at him again, that look of disapprobation tinged with faltering astonishment.

"What?" he said. "I'm sorry, I —"

Stella grimaced. "May I?" she said, and she placed the receiver back on its hook.

Immediately the telephone rang. The kitchen filled with a clangour of bells distinctly edged with barking dog. The dimmer, dire mantra of the barking seemed to entrance him, as though Fred were receiving a vision in and of sound whereby the whole world, the sum and detail of its awful intricacy, was being explicated. He pressed the heel of his hand to his forehead. His eyes met Stella's.

"Hadn't you better answer that?" she said.

He lifted the receiver and fitted it to his ear. After his initial hello the information came quickly, flowing through the instrument into the resonant pan of his skull.

"Say again," Fred said. "We have noise here. Could you please repeat that?"

The brisk interior voice repeated the facts, calmly yet swiftly, so there could be no mistaking.

Fred hung up the phone and turned slowly toward the bedrooms.

He spoke over his shoulder to Stella Smart: "We'll have to talk later. My mother's taken a turn."

Stella pocketed her tangle of keys and waited. Outside, the dog fell silent for a long, tense minute. Then it started again.

Late in the afternoon, returning along the river route, Fred studied the black clouds piling up to the southeast, clouds pent with rain, charged with thunder. If it broke, it would be the season's first. He felt the car shudder in the wind and he rolled down the window to let it blow in against his face. His mother was still alive, but just barely, hanging on by threads, and plainly she would never recognize him again. He drove slower, hungry to see chains of lightning fall to the dark, uneasy water. The sky loomed; the wind shook the budding trees. The weather was building slowly, the way it did in spring.

When he parked beside his mother's house it still hadn't broken. Gusts of warm air chased stray wrappers across the lawn. At once Fred noticed the dog's hut was empty; the meshed door banged slowly in the wind.

As he fitted the house key into the handle a movement in the backyard caught his attention. A flash of white beneath the hedge. He took a few steps closer. The raggedy, untrimmed tops of the cedar bushes waved like fingers. Between two bushes, just at ground level in the gap he'd created last summer, the neighbour's kid was trying to crawl through from the other side. His head and shoulders had made it, but the rest of him appeared to be stuck. The kid twisted onto his back and squirmed. Fred could almost read the pink lettering on the kid's stained white T-shirt. He moved closer. The kid was definitely stuck. For a moment Fred could hear him pant; then the breath caught in his fat chest as he strained to get out.

Fred took another step and looked down at the clear blue eyes that widened in the round, pale face.

"My dog got away!" the boy said. "I was chasing her through the bushes. She ran away through your bushes. I think my belt loop's caught."

Fred blinked, taking in the bag of potato chips mashed in the kid's chubby fist. In his strivings, the kid hadn't relinquished the chips.

"Well," said Fred, "I've warned you about this."

The kid heaved and gasped. His elbows flailed the matted April lawn. The grass, Fred reflected, was going to dirt and weeds. Sooner or later he would have to reseed it. Sooner or later someone would have to take care of things.

The kid became still again. "My dog ran away," he repeated. "She's worth lots of money. My dad will kill me if someone steals her."

"That dog? That dog's worth money?"

The kid lay there, trying to nod.

Fred closed his eyes and breathed in the information on the wind. He knew it would come now. Any minute. He hadn't done the weather these many years for nothing. He sat beside the kid and looked up at the cloud mass.

"What do you bet it will rain in the next three minutes?"

The kid, the fat half of him Fred could see, simulated a shrug. His eyes were on Fred.

"Let me tell you, friend. I know weather. Weather is one thing I know whereof I speak."

He realized that the fat kid's face contained an openness he hadn't expected. Beneath several layers of flesh was an aspect of blank acceptance that he had not noticed before.

Thunder rumbled beyond them and Fred scanned the horizon. When he looked again he saw that the kid was staring straight up, his eyes like little observation bubbles tilted toward the firmament.

"The first storm of the season is always something special," Fred told him. "This year it's come early."

The fat boy seemed to ponder this and it occurred to Fred that this kid on his back was in an ideal position to learn something. At this moment, pinned to the earth with atmospheric extremes impending, the fat boy was in the rare human state of being able to take something in, and if Fred, from the advantage of his years, had a fact or insight to pass along, now was the time.

He looked at the white, shaved head, at the eyes trained blankly on the heavens. Closer now, the thunder rumbled — not the definite crash that would clear the air, but a slow, ponderous vibration like a building collapsing. Fred imagined he could feel the vibration through the expectant earth. A thick drop of rain beaded on the boy's nascent forehead. Then another below the eye, streaking down the fat white cheek.

Fred sat beside him and watched the kid watch the sky that was changing above them. He tried to think of that most important thing he would tell him.

THE DREAM OF PHILIP II

It was two days after Christmas, deep in the layered blue freeze of mid-afternoon, when Marnie rang the doorbell. I'd been sitting at the kitchen table with an open book, watching my coffee get cold, wondering about certain people I'd once known intimately who were now complete strangers. The bell chimed two tones and I rose half dazed and opened the door. She started talking immediately, a girlish figure in striped tights and her boyfriend's parka, her arms wrapped around skis and poles. A few yards down the driveway a clean, white car purred in park; white exhaust plumes rising in the sharp, crystalline air. A woman I didn't know sat behind the wheel.

"I forgot my apartment keys at my Mom's place," Marnie said. "That's her in the car." We both looked and the woman behind the wheel waved. "Can I wait here with my stuff until

Rip gets home? He's coming this evening. I just need a place to wait a few hours."

She brought the skis inside and we went out to unload the car. Marnie introduced me to her mother and then we carried her suitcases and books inside. Finally, we hauled in a large painted canvas and a statue, the heavy clay bust of a woman. We sat it on the couch, where it made severe dents in the cushions and stared unhappily into space.

"Not like that," Marnie said. "I don't want it to topple or anything."

She lifted the bust with a little grunt and laid it on its back near the ski equipment and the canvas. The painting depicted the naked lower half of a large-hipped woman; I asked Marnie if the hips could be joined to the sculpted torso to make a complete person.

"As if you knew art," she said, collapsing on the couch where the statue had been. "Oh man, I'm beat." Her striped legs sprawled from the open parka. She blinked at her wet boots and popped back to her feet.

"David, can I bring my mother in for awhile?"

"Certainly. Sure. Would she like coffee?"

"Maybe. Or tea. She might want tea."

Marnie bustled out the door and I put water in the kettle. In a moment she returned with her mother, a trim little woman in a pink track outfit. They took off their shoes and Marnie dropped her coat on the floor.

They both said, "Brrr!" and made straight for the couch, where they curled up on either side, their feet nearly touching, Marnie's striped foot an inch from her mother's blue one.

"This is an interesting house," her mother said, looking around.

"David sold his car last month to make the mortgage payment."

They both smiled at me pleasantly.

"I haven't really decorated or anything," I said. "For some reason I've never gotten around to that."

"Rip and I decided not to hang any art that wasn't original."

I pointed: "That's an El Greco. What makes you think it's not original?"

Marnie laughed. She said, "But there's something creepy about it. I mean, for the setting. You know? It's an unusual picture to hang in the living-room."

Marnie's mother regarded her with disinterest. Although they might have been mother and daughter to the casual eye, to me that fact was not obvious. Marnie's hair was a tangle of black around large, startled eyes; her small face, pale and freckled, with a provocative dot that touched a peak of her upper lip, made the picture of a brainy waif. Her mother was similarly slight but with most of the insouciance ironed out: more determined than resigned. Her hair was a strawberry-blonde dye that almost matched her outfit. The three of us, I reckoned, were more or less evenly staggered in age, with me in the middle and ten years, more or less, on either side.

"I know," I said, as their attention shifted to the front window, "the 'burbs are awful. But it's quiet here. And I don't feel any pressure to be chummy with the neighbours. They move in and out pretty frequently."

"David's a disc jockey," Marnie said. "He has hundreds of old records."

"Program director, actually," I said. "Plus, I have a show on Sunday nights. It keeps me amused."

Her mother rose and said, "I'd better get back on the road. I have a party this evening."

On her way out the door she reached into her purse and brought out a book of coupons. She thrust them into Marnie's hand.

"Here," she said. "These are for restaurants. They must have these places around here."

Marnie glanced through the coupons. "I never go to them," she said. "I don't eat that stuff."

"Take David out. It's almost free."

She pumped my hand and hugged Marnie. "Use those coupons," she said.

After she left Marnie shrugged and shook her head.

"My poor mother. On the way here I got so mad at her. She never listens. She has no idea who I am."

"They never do," I said, and Marnie rose up on her toes and kissed me.

"Make me some tea," she said.

We settled in at the oval table where I'd been reading and drifting half an hour earlier. She described her Christmas in particular terms: the big white bed in the papered room of her grandfather's house, the boring gifts, and one transcendent moment on her way to church when an ancient woman slipped and shot into the street like a carved ivory ski. She told how the traffic screeched and her mother gasped, and another old woman whooped like crazy to see her sister slice through the intersection, fast and unimpeded.

"Luckily, no one was hurt," Marnie said. She sipped noisily from her teacup. Frowning slightly, she turned the saucer over to check the manufacturer's mark. She set cup and saucer on the table again. "I'm so tired," she said.

"When's Rip getting in?"

"Around dinner time. I called him from a gas station on the highway and told him about the keys. He'll phone here, don't worry."

Boyfriend Rip is a portly young customs broker, not precisely at one with his dashing name. Barely twenty-three, he seems just now to be graduating to the sedentary life which had been his goal since his teens. I like Rip. One day, over lunch in town, he confided to me that one of his fondest longings concerned the hot turkey sandwich with mashed potatoes served at a local diner. He said that there were times in the office when his business mind went blank and the urgent math of his afternoon was suddenly replaced by the steaming vision of that open-faced sandwich smothered in hot, pale gravy. He portrayed this dish so lovingly, so vividly, that I made a point of trying it a day or two later. And he was right. It was an exceptional turkey sandwich.

Marnie played with her teacup and moaned. "What a wasted holiday. My mother might take me to Martinique in February. Oh David, I'm so fucking tired." She glanced up with wide dark eyes, her hair in her face. "I should quit swearing," she said.

Not long ago I'd told her that I'd noticed her generation — people in their 20's — swore a lot more than mine. Of course, I swore more than my elders, but Marnie and her friends had taken it a step further. They were especially fond, I observed, of *fucking* as an adjective. It was just a passing comment, but I think it made her uncomfortable. I think she thought I was judging.

"I could use a nap," she said. "This time in winter always makes me tired. No, it makes me dreamy. I have my best dreams on afternoons like this."

The light through the living-room window was deepening, blue to violet-grey, and the street lay frozen and silent in post-Christmas gloom. In a few days people would start dragging out their half-dead trees, sticking them in snowbanks or just leaving them like carcasses in mats of needles beside their porches and driveways.

"Let's take a nap, David. Let's just lie down for awhile. I have to close my eyes for an hour or I'll lose my mind."

She pushed back her chair and came around the table, smiling like someone enduring pain, until I stood and we climbed the stairs, side by side.

The room was grey and getting cold; I started to draw the curtains and she said, "No, I like to see the sky while I'm falling asleep in the afternoon." She burrowed under the blankets and I got on the bed beside her. "Aren't you getting under the covers? It's cold, David. Come on and get in."

I slipped beneath the blankets on the oversized bed in the small, darkening room. I said, "This bed is like some leaky old boat left over from a long-ago war."

Marnie giggled and burrowed deeper, pressing her back against me.

We lay still for a minute. I said, "I have a hard time sleeping during the day. I can't relax. And I never dream. Not during daylight."

"Just don't speak. Close your eyes and be quiet and soon you'll drop off."

"I don't think so."

"Just be quiet," she said.

I turned toward her and she pressed closer, facing the wall. I slid my arm under hers and sort of held her, breathing in and out in unison. I tried to recollect a time when sleeping with someone was habitual, the warm melding of random thoughts, the worries and regimens tapering together and receding from the workday like sea foam sliding off hard wet sand. I tried to remember Jillian, who was exactly my age, the nights we spent in various beds and how uneasily we fit, as if our quotidian thoughts came from separate worlds and our minds could not dream in the other's proximity. Truth is, I can recollect those nights because my sleep was so thin and brittle beside her. I recall the beds, the walls, those summer dawnings wide awake with my eyes closed, excruciatingly aware of the distance between us on all planes.

But the wonder of Marnie was that she had already dozed off, making a soft, plosive sound with each exhalation through puckered lips. And though I might have responded to some friendly necking, I was pleased, even flattered, that she could subside against me in this oblivious and trusting manner. After all my complicated histories of sleep and beds, it did not displease me to feel this round, girlish body respiring with little sighs against my chest and legs.

There was a golden day back in the fall when Marnie materialized at the radio station and announced that she was taking me to lunch. We drove out to a Greek restaurant near my place and watched the corporate types hunkering down to souvlaki and beer. In the lobby, a red-faced man in a sheeny suit presented Marnie with his company card, as if it were an invitation to a ball. During dessert she pointed my attention toward another man dining alone beside a miniature tree. He had been a professor of hers and she told the story of how he had invited her to a party at his country house. When she arrived there were no other guests, only Marnie and this reptilian academic who got her high and made vague propositions. Now that I know her better I understand the meaning of this story, how it parallels the dense narratives of her dreams, which she tells compulsively. But that day, that brisk and sparkling afternoon in October, the story served to intensify the laughter and complicity between us. After lunch we drove back to my place and sat on the couch, kissing happily. She unbuttoned her shirt and let me kiss her breasts, which were small and white and oddly cool in my palms. Without warning she broke away and moaned, "Oh, poor Rip." Abruptly, she became businesslike, glancing at her watch, grabbing for her coat. In fifteen minutes she had me back at the station.

I shifted slightly and rolled my shoulder for circulation.

What Marnie's about, who she is, is not defined simply, but her steady breathing, her physical peace beside me on the bed, slowly affected my own breath and heart, and eventually I slept.

She woke me when she turned on her back and exclaimed, "Oh man, what a dream I had! I dreamed about Caitlin Ranny, the clerk at the bookstore. I dreamed she was going down on me. You know Caitlin, the one with all that glorious blonde hair..."

Funny thing was, I don't usually dream — at least, I don't remember my dreams — but as Marnie told hers I realized that I had dreamed also. In the short hour of sleep beside Marnie I had dreamed of Jillian's sixteen-year-old daughter, Angela. I hadn't consciously thought of Angela in months, but this dream was like turning a corner and meeting a long-lost relative or friend. It was hard to say, and I didn't try to say it, not to Marnie, but in the dream Angela was showing me through a series of caves cast in an icy blue light. Her demeanour was altered; she spoke brightly and moved with animal-like swiftness and decision, not at all the introverted and often sulky girl I remembered. But this was undeniably Angela, who broke two and a half years of silent neutrality on my relation to her mother to tell me about the other man who had started coming to their house. In life she delivered this information with her face averted, almost in passing, as I waited for her mother to come down the stairs. But in the dream Angela and I were cronies, partners in adventure, exploring the underground labyrinth. She led me by the hand or scampered ahead, entering each new cavern with an excitement and delight that outshone the last. She laughed and called back for me to hurry, and each new space held a light that was lovelier, more brilliant with higher blue, than the one we'd just left.

"I have a major crush on her," Marnie said. "I keep thinking up excuses to buy books." She sighed and pulled her hand through her tangled black hair.

The phone rang and I swung my legs into the dark. It rang again while I felt my way down the stairs to the kitchen.

"I thought nobody was there," he said. Through the static his voice was strained and high, and I didn't immediately know him. Then he asked for Marnie.

"Rip. Where are you?"

"Last stop on the 401. Absolutely the worst drive of my life. Blowing snow and the heater quit. Marnie's there, right?"

For some reason I wanted to stay on another minute. It was strange, standing there in the house that had gone dark around us, the transition from sleep to Rip's voice coming in from beyond. The familiar rooms felt transfigured by the streetlight shining through the window in the front room. Rip's voice seemed to connect and circumscribe everything in a vivid, blue space. For a change, I felt perfectly positioned in that space, satisfied that I wasn't on the road, but sympathetic to Rip out there in the cold.

"Here," Marnie said, suddenly beside me in the dark, reaching for the phone.

I went into the other room and looked out at the wind-smoothed snow while her voice chattered up and down the scales. The street was empty and white and nobody had turned their Christmas lights on. Then I drew the curtains and switched on a lamp. I turned up the thermostat and put an old Art Tatum record on the stereo. The music mixed happily, lazily, with the warm lamplight and Marnie's driven voice.

Later, after we loaded her skis and things into the cab and it pulled into the street, I still felt calm and satisfied.

The week passed swiftly, oddly, without the work hours making any particular impression on my conscious thoughts. The intense cold sat implacable on the town; an unnatural calm presided over a clear and motionless landscape. Friday I finished work early. Walking from the bus-stop to the convenience store on the corner, I saw a large hawk gliding over the suburbs, looking for food or warmth or both. It floated bonily over the neat bungalows and semi-detached units, a feathered cross in the frigid blue sky. As I watched it I could easily imagine these houses as vacant monuments to a time and manner that had utterly vanished.

Next morning a dark western sky turned into a winter storm: a few bitter flakes, then a full-fledged blizzard with a hard white wind that blew around the streetlamps like angry surf. In the weekend paper there was a terse piece about the closing of the local art museum — Jillian's museum. She'd served as primary curator for almost ten years and during her tenure the institution had achieved significant gains. But recently, according to the article, funding from all levels had been slashed. In a nasty fight with the city council the museum's trustees threw in the towel, which the city promptly accepted. Now Jillian and her staff were gone.

The snow fell and flew, blotting out the world. I walked around the house staring out at it. My radio show was that night, and normally the thought of going out in bad weather would have worried me, but I kept thinking about Jillian, who had changed her life several times over since I met her; how she'd become synonymous with her job and its illusion of mission, how her identity had melded with the building itself, its marbled lobbies and warm fluorescent workrooms. I tried to imagine her back in her house, sending Angela to school, reheating her coffee in the microwave, sitting down at the computer to rework her resumé. There she was, a woman in mid-life who had pursued her career with that half-manic second wind people get once they have decided that career is everything, that work alone counts. I thought about her business wardrobe and the floppy disks she'd had to leave in the office. I also thought about Marnie, working part-time at the daycare centre; how she probably loved Rip in her own way. I considered what love meant when you're semi-employed and in your twenties. There was a Sunday last autumn when she and I stepped out of a café in the city and I spotted Jillian across the street. Marnie seemed taken aback that I'd ever had access to this hip-looking, handsome woman in leather and jeans. "Wow," Marnie said, "that's how I want to end up. Like her." And it seemed to me that Marnie treated me with new respect or interest.

As the snow lashed the house, I thought about Marnie and Jillian in their homes right now: Marnie with Rip, watching videos; Jillian and her daughter making hot chocolate in the kitchen, and the snow flying like TV static in the silences between us. I parted the curtains and looked out in the dying light: far down the street a single obscured figure fought through the blizzard, and it struck me: there are people out there.

My show at the station runs from eight until midnight, and I play anything that moves me — jazz, funk, classical. That Sunday I had nothing to say, no energy to project through the microphone, so I ran the entirety of Mahler's 6th. The building was mostly empty and I sat in the studio with the lights down, drinking coffee, listening to the music. When the damn thing was over I got on the air and apologized to the world. Like God making up to Noah after the flood, I promised I'd never play that music again. And as a token of penance I finished off the evening with James Brown, Al Green, and "The Tighten Up."

The taxi ride home was frantic, with a hard slanting snow that came at the high beams like tracer bullets. The driver wheeled through giddy skids and slides in his shirtsleeves, an old scarf wrapped around his head. I gave him a big tip and apologized for bringing him out on such a night. He grunted and said, "At least you're sober."

The wind grabbed me the moment I stepped out of the car. I struggled with the key and fell into the cold dark of the front room: immediately I realized the phone was ringing and I rushed to it, breathing hard and trailing snow.

It was Marnie.

"Oh good, you're home." She spoke in a low, little-girl whisper. "Rip is in the tub and I wanted to talk to you."

"The tub? This time of night?"

"He takes a hot bath when he can't sleep. He's wound pretty tight. What's wrong?"

"I just got in."

"Oh. Should I call back?"

"That's all right."

"Actually" — and here her voice became almost inaudible — "I want you to come to dinner Friday night. Rip's going away on business and I'm inviting you and Caitlin. We can smoke the dope Rip gave me for my birthday…"

She went on in that breathless whisper. I loosened my overcoat and leaned against the kitchen table, the snow pooling at my feet.

Suddenly, in an attractive panic, she said, "Rip's out of the tub! I have to go!"

She made a kissing sound and the line went dead.

Later, I reread a letter she'd sent last fall from New York, where she'd gone on holiday with Rip. It was written in her tiny script on Plaza Hotel stationery. Like her phone calls, the letter conveyed its message in thrilled whispers while Rip was engaged elsewhere. She wrote that she absolutely could not get involved with me at this stage in her life. She also mentioned that she imagined me when she was having sex with Rip.

I folded the letter into its creamy, emblazoned envelope and went to bed.

Rip's a good guy, a likeable head, but somehow it's hard to think of him. In many ways, he doesn't seem to exist. The fact that I've got more than ten years on him is only part of it. And it's not like Marnie and I are having a bona fide affair. In fact, that's precisely the problem. If sex were involved, we'd be selling him out for a currency everybody deals in, a commodity that makes the world go round. That I could understand. It happens. But this other stuff. This emotional leak and bleed that goes nowhere. It's slow death, a creeping burn. Like selling your birthright for nickels and dimes.

But maybe what Marnie does is what everybody does. The way of the world. That was Jillian's phrase. It's what she did when she worked until midnight three or four times a week. It's what even Angela understood when she told me about the man who had replaced me in their lives, just as I had replaced the man who came after her father. The way of the world. There's a whole world in that phrase and I've never quite known what to make of it.

Friday night I took a bus into town and disembarked about two blocks from the building where Rip and Marnie lived. After days of hiding from the snow and cold it felt good to be outside, on the street, a steady stream of cars breaking up the darkness around me. The unshovelled walkway to their front entrance was strewn with flyers frozen solid. I pushed the button and presently Marnie appeared, squinting behind the glass.

She opened the door and said, "Exquisite timing, as usual."

"Meaning?"

"Don't ask. Look, David: Caitlin's up there and we're pretty stoned. Just go with the flow, okay? Can you do that for me?"

"Go with the flow. I can do that."

She waggled up the stairway and I followed on the trace of her perfume. She was done up in a summery beach outfit: Hawaiian silk shirt, baggy shorts and sandals, her arms and legs very white against the brightly coloured fabrics. The apartment was one of two on the fifth and final floor. At least five pairs of Rip's shoes were lined up outside their door as if they were loyally awaiting his return. A notice taped on the wall above them read, WILL THE PERSON WHO TOOK MY WINGTIPS PLEASE RETURN THEM TO THIS SPOT.

Marnie held the door and motioned me inside.

I left my coat on a peg and followed her into the kitchen. A young woman about Marnie's age stood beside the refrigerator with a wine glass in her hand. She wore one face of boredom over another of peering intensity. Or vice versa, one face masking the other. On first impression, I couldn't say which face, the blank or the intent one, was the true colour of the actual person.

"At last you meet David," Marnie said to her, and the other woman swung her head to give me the full effect of her hair, a fall of straight whitish blonde that glittered across her black turtleneck. Her slacks were grey and loose, almost drab.

"Maybe you've met Caitlin somewhere," Marnie said.

Caitlin looked out at me through her hair. Her features were rigid and fine. I couldn't decide if she was inscrutable, or just stoned.

"Let's finish that joint before we eat," Marnie said.

She led us toward the larger room, sandals flapping. "What a day. I ought to be ashamed," she said.

"Eighteen days and I'm gone," Caitlin said. "I can tell Locklin what to do with his store and his job."

"Caitlin's quitting work next month," Marnie told me. "She's getting out of here."

"Where are you going?" I asked.

"Somewhere far away."

"Djibouti," Marnie said.

"Good choice. Where's Djibouti?"

Marnie lifted the joint from a ceramic ashtray and handed it to me. She struck a match; I inclined my head toward her hand and took a drag.

"Hey," she said. "Let's get wrecked and watch *Star Trek*."

I passed the joint to Caitlin. She held it like a cigarette and inhaled silently.

"Unless David wants to eat," Marnie said. "Sometimes he gets cranky when we put off food for TV."

"So long as we eat eventually."

"We'll eat," Marnie said, and she doubled with laughter. She straightened and wiped her eye. "Oh God. I'm fucked."

She lifted the remote and levelled it at the big free-standing screen. It filled with colour and sound. Immediately we found seats: Marnie and Caitlin on the couch. I took the easy chair in the corner.

"Oh hell," Marnie said, cruising the dial.

"There it is," I said. "You passed it."

"That's the old one. We want *The Next Generation*."

The stations flipped soundlessly, easily, like bright signs zipping past on the freeway. Watching them, I felt like I was travelling, covering ground, flying low in an airplane that couldn't decide whether to take off or touch down.

"Damn it," Marnie said, giving the wand angry little shakes as she sped through the dial.

"Look," I said. "There's another *Star Trek*."

"But that's *Star Trek II*, the movie!"

Caitlin let her head loll so her hair completely hid her face. Then she looked up and her hair shifted, a pattern like clear light on wind-ruffled waters. I handed the joint to her.

"It'll be on soon," Marnie said. "Let's just watch this."

It was a commercial for natural cough drops. A casually dressed man on a Swiss mountain called the name of the product into the valleys and peaks. The name rolled and resonated throughout the world, three smooth syllables like the secret name of God.

Something else came on. I looked at Caitlin. I said, "I really don't know where Djibouti is."

Marnie laughed. "Hey Caitlin. David's jammed."

Caitlin stared at the screen through her bright, streaming hair and I saw her face carved in marble, gazing up from the bottom of a clear, cold river that rushed through the mountains.

Marnie popped to her feet, still grasping the remote.

"Don't let it start without me," she said. She handed the remote to Caitlin and went out to the hallway.

Without turning her attention from the screen, Caitlin said, "So where did you meet Rip?"

I thought for a moment. "I honestly can't remember," I said.

"He has lots of respect for you. He says you understand Marnie and their relationship."

Marnie came back and flounced down on the couch.

"Has it started? All right. Nothing's happened." She tucked her feet behind the cushions and put on her glasses. "Pay attention, David. Someday this program will come in handy, socially. You'll land a job or a lover by being Trek-wise. Sixties people do it with the old show."

"Sixties people never watched the old show," I said.

"You should know," she replied.

I looked at Caitlin. "I'm not Sixties," I said. "I came later."

"What about Jillian? How old was she?"

"Same as me. But she was different. She slipped into the fast track easily."

The show began and nobody spoke. Caitlin sat beside Marnie on the couch with the remote placed deliberately between them. During the first commercial the dope was relit and passed around.

"Does anyone have the munchies?" I said.

"Shush. I want to hear this."

We sat around the set and watched the adventure in space.

Although a few of the characters were physically grotesque, and nearly all had endured extreme dangers and upsets, everyone on the starship was civilized and polite — too polite — like a race of exiled ophthalmologists, thoroughly versed in the vicissitudes of cramped, modern living.

The screen flickered and changed hues. Marnie watched absorbedly. I couldn't tell if Caitlin cared one way or another. Her face betrayed nothing: all the passion of her being seemed to reside in her hair. That's what I thought as we watched the elegant humans and well-spoken grotesques wend their way through fantastic displays of intergalactic power and light — that the sum and zenith of Caitlin's energy flowed back and forth through her hyperbolic blonde hair.

"I hope we're going to eat soon," I said.

"Just wait. This is almost over."

"Where did these people learn to act? Instead of drama they have facial cartilage."

Marnie frowned. "Rip has a theory. He says he'd like to write a Ph.D. about the architecture of the Enterprise. Not just all the great machines in it, but how living for months in all those interconnected decks and pulsing corridors impacts on humans."

Finally it was over and Marnie killed the picture.

She sighed and leaned her head on Caitlin's shoulder. "David, why don't you get us some more wine."

I blinked and thought about moving. "All right," I said. "Who wants more wine?"

I got up and collected their glasses and went out to the kitchen. It was a student's apartment, with political posters and empty beer bottles; no sign of the sculpture or canvas we'd loaded into the cab. I poured the wine from a large bottle on the counter and started back with a full glass in either hand. Caitlin met me in the narrow hallway.

"Nobody drinks white anymore," I said.

She stood slightly slouched, beautiful and inert in her plain black sweater. With an odd, ducking gesture she glanced over her shoulder and leaned toward me.

"I think she knows," she said. Her voice was bland, almost inflectionless. "I think Rip told her about him and me."

I stood there holding the wine glasses.

"He told me you knew. So Marnie must, too. If you know, she knows. She's fucking with my head. She's fucking with both of us."

She directed her hair over her shoulders and away from her face with both hands. Her neck was blotched and speckled, a reaction to the dope or wine, maybe. There seemed to be a white noise around her face, like running water or static.

"I guess I'm pretty stoned," I said.

She took the wine glasses from my hands and disappeared down the hallway. I poured some for myself in a plastic cup and joined them in the other room. It was dark, save for two squat, black candles sputtering on a bookshelf. Caitlin sat on the floor, her back against the couch. Marnie had stretched out with her head and shoulders on Caitlin's lap.

"That bastard Locklin," Marnie blurted. "If he so much as touched me I'd feed him to the cops."

"It's not that concrete. Nothing that would stick."

"Still. What a creep."

Caitlin's hair drifted across Marnie's face. She sighed and lifted her chin to take it like sunlight.

"What about dinner?" I said.

Nobody spoke. Caitlin's finger described tiny circles on the inside of Marnie's upturned wrist.

"Oh man," Marnie said, "I have to tell you guys about this dream I had last night. No, two nights ago. I dreamed Caitlin and I were flying to Rio or Martinique, somewhere warm and blue. And Rip was supposed to be with us. But somehow he missed the plane, and it was just Caitlin and me, in our seats snoozing."

She told this dream in a happy voice, chirping along, with her eyes serenely shut. Caitlin watched her face while she rubbed Marnie's wrist.

"Mmm…" Marnie said, "that's nice. That's nice."

She went on about the dream. She stopped and opened her eyes.

"I've forgotten a part. Oh shit, I forgot something."

"Get it right," Caitlin said. Her hand moved from Marnie's wrist to her collar, playing with the bright silk.

"In the middle of the flight, while we were eating or watching a movie, I looked out, and there was Rip! Clinging to the wing! He was laid out in the wind, holding on for his life."

"What was the movie?" Caitlin asked.

"What?"

"The movie. Can you remember the movie on the plane?"

Marnie laughed and pressed her face into Caitlin's lap. One of the candles went out. Marnie reached up and touched a strand of Caitlin's hair. She pulled it gently through her fingers again and again.

"I like hearing dreams," Caitlin said. "They can mean everything or nothing. Let's hear another. David should tell us one."

"David doesn't dream," Marnie said.

"It's true."

"Everybody dreams," said Caitlin. "You just don't remember."

"I get dreams confused with what actually happened. I've probably had them, but I honestly can't tell them from real life."

Marnie turned her face from side to side so Caitlin's hair brushed her forehead.

Caitlin said, "I used to get this nightmare that a free-floating camera was following me everywhere I went. Once a month, maybe, I had that dream."

"I'd like to put that camera on you in Africa," Marnie said. "I'd like to see what happens over there."

"I hope it's good," Caitlin said.

We were quiet again. For no good reason I recollected an early *Star Trek* episode in which Abraham Lincoln appears in outerspace. He's just sitting out there, like the monument in D.C., frowning beneath his stovepipe hat. I wanted to tell the women about it, but this too seemed more like something I might have dreamed. The more I thought about it the less certain I became that this was something I'd actually seen.

Stretched across Caitlin's lap, Marnie appeared to be sleeping. I kept my eye on the candle's small flame. It squirmed like a white worm on a hook, a unit of pure pain that couldn't die fast enough. Marnie sighed, and when I looked, Caitlin was bending close to her, the white-blonde hair hiding their faces, falling over them in satiny plaits and ribbons.

I stood then, watching for another moment. Marnie's small, pale hand cupped Caitlin's shoulder and I heard a faint gasp like a child's.

I went out to the hall and gathered my coat from the hook. I closed the door behind me and stepped past the row of Rip's shoes on the landing. With my hand on the rail, I took the stairs in twos, down to the brightly lit entrance and outside, into the sudden cold. The buses had stopped running and there were no cars in sight. At the blinking red signal I crossed and turned down a side street lined with sombre, older houses that stood shoulder-to-shoulder in the winter dark. A solitary set of footprints wound through the new, ankle-deep snow ahead of me, and I had the sense that someone I knew was out there, hurrying on, just out of sight. I began to run, taking my hands from my pockets, pumping my arms. Someone I had just missed was making tracks down the street of darkened houses, gaining speed as I increased mine.

I ran through the blue snow and heard the muffled footsteps in front of me moving faster, then faster, leading me deeper into the maze of this place.

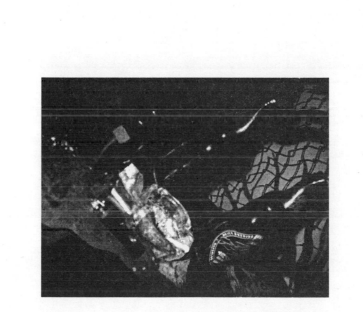

FLAMINGO: PART TWO

Around 6:30 Arthur pulled into the parking lot beside the mall. The day had been mild and overcast, full of last-minute errands and arrangements and sudden, soft showers that seemed to come down in odd dashes, then long drones, like some kind of April code. He got out and locked the door and breathed the humid thrill of the spring air. At last, after the long and heavy winter, the world was starting to change. He'd pick up his groceries, stash them in the car, and hike across the parking lot to Rosemary's building. Maybe he could talk to her. Maybe he could make her see that this trip to California was just a vacation that would return him to a better frame of mind.

As he entered the lower level through a bank of glass doors he decided to pick up a few pens and a new sketch book at the office supply store on the other side of the mall. Then he'd come back for the groceries. If he had enough money left, some flowers for Rosemary might be a good idea. Flowers made her quiet and glad, every time. They touched her in a way that in turn touched him. Watching her face softly shine over the flowers brought his heart to his throat. In spite of all the trouble in her life, she still reacted to the right bouquet. When he asked himself why he kept on with her, this was one of the reasons.

The lower level was oddly empty. A few couples strolling absent-mindedly; some teenagers slouching toward the exits. The long sprawls of glass and tile produced a cavernous silence, like an empty train station with odd echoes in the corners. He glanced up at the second level: one old man with his arms folded on the chrome rail stared blankly down. The signs and neons in the shop windows on both floors struck Arthur as peculiarly non-commercial. On a vacant night like this they might have been vitrines for strange reptiles that slept unseen beneath piles of merchandise.

Since Rose had moved last summer into the stark, mono-lithic complex across the way he had spent far more time in the mall than he'd ever thought possible. He hated malls. Who didn't? But this was where Rose came to buy food and baubles, little jars of skin cream and bath beads and perfumes that made her life bearable. Many an argument had been walked off in here, finished with coffee and muffins in one of the food court concessions. Just a month ago at Saint Cinnamon's they sat at a little round table and she wrote something on a napkin and pushed it around the danish they were sharing. He'd started to read it aloud and she put a fin-ger to her lips. On the napkin, beneath the device of the car-toon devil, she'd written: *My building is under police surveil-lance.* She smiled and held the finger to her lips. He smiled and folded it into his shirt pocket. Like so many of her hints and insinuations, he hadn't dared to ask. He still had the napkin at home. He didn't know why he saved it. He'd had the uneasy feeling that it might mean something to him over time, that it might function as evidence of a sort after some larger, inevitable drama concluded.

Recollecting the napkin did not please him, and he walked faster toward the stationery store, the muzak moving above and around him like a cold, mentholated draft.

As he moved to the far end of the mall he saw figures sitting around a small table set up outside the department store, kitty-corner to the shop where he intended to buy the sketchbook. In the next instant, he recognized Jean, then Rosemary, then a bearded man in a suit, all seated on folding chairs around the table. Their presence here, he began to remember, was connected with some project for the United Way where Jean worked and Rosemary went in one or two days a week on a volunteer basis. As he approached, Rosemary's face came up with a crooked smile. She was dressed to the nines, in heels and a bright filmy dress; her hair was done up and she wore a sheer, purplish scarf around her neck.

"Hey, hey," Jean said. "The Artmeister's here."

She had an almost masculine poise and large, droll eyes that mostly matched her character. More than ten years younger than Rose, she had nonetheless taken her under her wing, getting her involved in United Way fundraisers, introducing her to people in the business community who might help her land a job down the line.

"Hello Arthur," Rosemary said, with pointed formality in her rich English voice. He had started across to kiss her, but something in her tone checked him, and instead he gave her shoulder an awkward squeeze. For a moment he stood before the small arc of chairs, the trio looking up at him, the yellow light spangling the silver kettles and china plates in the store behind them. Then Jean introduced the man as Gordon LaChance, a name that Arthur knew belonged to this year's honorary executive of the United Way. One night back in October Rosemary had phoned from a downtown restaurant where the office was having a party and mentioned how she'd been introduced to the new chairman. Arthur couldn't recall if it was that night or later when she'd described LaChance as a sharp businessman with a silk suit and a neatly trimmed beard. In fact, the guy was nothing more than an appliance salesman at another mall — Arthur had heard his commercials on the radio — but the detail of the beard stuck in his mind unpleasantly.

Gordon LaChance reached up to Arthur without rising from his seat. They shook hands and Arthur dropped into an empty chair beside Jean, the chair farthest away from Rose.

"Is it raining out there?" LaChance asked him.

"It stopped just as I parked. But it might have started again."

"Thank God winter is over," Rosemary said. "I thought it would never end. I thought I would perish from the boredom of it all."

She spoke in a fluttery rush, working up her emotion. Arthur could see that she was after something. He could see that she was here on a mission. She pressed a hand to her throat and affected a shudder. The others watched her and waited expectantly. Rose seemed to lose her thought and lowered her head; she gazed at the floor and smiled mysteriously.

Jean said, "Business was brisk this morning. But tonight it's off. I don't know what's going on. This place is dead."

She went on to explain the point of the exhibit to Arthur, how the department store was donating a percentage of the day's profits to the United Way. He glanced at the pamphlets on the table, the various forms for those interested in learning or giving more. He looked around the mall, which was polished and empty, just a few shoppers moving down toward the food court. It seemed to him a shapeless shadow floated above this place, as if it had its own weather, its own peculiar seasons which came and went on the darker dynamics that constituted its meaning.

Rosemary said, "I just wandered over from my building. I fed the kids and thought, 'Time to get out and give the troops moral support.' What a day. You should have seen what

Talbott wore to school."

The others looked at her as she rambled on about this and that, her voice moving up and down, circling the little group in the sterile space like a flock of pink birds going around faster and faster.

Arthur sat back in the chair and held a breath. The sound system was playing "It's my party and I'll cry if I want to..." Innocently enough he had wandered into something. Again. Now he'd have to wait and watch it play itself out.

He blinked and realized that LaChance had asked him a question.

"I'm sorry —"

"Arthur just quit his job at Computrax," Rose said, almost angrily. "Now he's going to California to paint the ocean."

LaChance kept looking at him.

"Things piled up. It was a lousy job," Arthur said. "You know how it gets. It was just database. It got so nothing felt real."

As he spoke he realized he was talking on the wrong plane. Inadvertently he'd opened himself in a way that was not appropriate to a Tuesday night in the mall. Before he could fix it, Rosemary said:

"In two days he'll be on the other end of the continent."

As she spoke he watched the crooked smile, her mouth gripping the sentence with bitter resolve. Her tension seemed to match the odd light, the hollowness at the centre of this centreless place.

He said, "You talk as though I'm never coming back."

LaChance shook his head. "You wouldn't catch me going anywhere they have earthquakes. You'd have to be crazy to live where they have earthquakes."

"More people die from the cold every winter right here," Arthur said. "Statistically, life is far riskier in the north."

LaChance leaned forward, his elbows on his knees and his hands folded.

"Those are just the stupid people," he said.

"But who wants to live where there are so many of them?"

The women stared and immediately Arthur added, "No, you're right. It's just a matter of time before The Big One. I went to university out there and I'd like to go back and see it again. I want to see if I'm remembering it right."

LaChance loosened his tie. Arthur could see that the other man hadn't been apprised of his relation to Rosemary. He could see that Rose, in some kind of panic, had decided to show LaChance her moves.

"Actually," Arthur went on, "my family comes from this town way back. Go down to the old cemetery and you can find them, dating back well over a hundred years. The first ones were Johnsons, I think."

Rosemary showed them her lovely, broken smile. Johnson was one of her assumed names, and they'd often joked about how she had bridged those famous degrees of separation in a single stroke. A neighbour in her building, a retired man who lived across the hall, was also named Johnson, and the joy the old gent took in fancying Rosemary a long-lost daughter was something that perpetually amused her, though Arthur sensed a sadness behind her mirth, as if she would gladly accept this proper old man as her guardian and grandfather to her children if he would take on the horrors of her past. And the irony of having the most common name in the world while being related to nobody, being utterly without kin and connection, was not lost on her.

An awkward silence fell over the group and they stared out into the vacant mall as though entranced by the vacancy and silence.

"I'd better get my groceries," Arthur said, rising from his chair. "I'll get my things and come back. Won't be long."

They watched him go with static smiles. Rosemary's face, he noted, was pale and strained. Her smile, with its beguiling but undeniably fractured quality, should have declared trouble to the alert observer. She came from an old and nearly extinct school of theatrical beauties who had little faith in any of their personal powers other than sheer physical appeal, having seen how it made things jump. Right now, back near the department store, she would be flashing her best angles and lines, raising her chin, crossing her legs. Would LaChance guess that something was amiss? Could an appliance salesman see the broken glass in that smile? If she finagled a date would she get around to telling him her story, not the intoxicating stories of her girlhood abroad, but the impossible-to-sort chronology of criminal husbands and random lovers who had consumed the better parts of her youth? The casually met men who gave her fur coats and short drunken trips in luxury automobiles? Would she show him her wallet full of aliases and business cards from Federal agents who still phoned her at midnight just to shoot the breeze?

Only now, walking through the mall, Arthur realized the significance of how she'd told him the worst of her history during their first night together, so the story of one passion got told while another passion was in progress, as if it were all the same drug and she was hopelessly addicted...

What had he been thinking, going into that place? The facts were there in the dark around them, with ghastly faces from her other lives watching from the shadows. But the action in that room was so intense, so stark and elemental, that he had ignored everything but the woman who cried and struggled and cajoled him.

He struck this thought, this image, and kept walking.

But what the hell was Rosemary doing? She might at least talk to him before she went after another man. She had asked him once, "Do you think that I'm immoral?" He'd thought about it and replied, "For you the term doesn't apply." But in his clearest mind he knew she was afflicted with a desperate predilection toward the things that had derailed her in the first place. One day, driving into town and apropos of nothing they'd been talking about, she announced that she'd been featured in several pornographic movies. They were waiting for the light at the corner of King and West streets, and his mind went blank. He could only nod while Rose explained how her mob-connected husband had doped her and pimped her to his cronies. She hastened to say that all of them had been business executives, erstwhile pillars of the economy, a detail that dismayed Arthur as much as the actual fact of her participation. He'd intended to ask her why she'd told him this part of her past; he'd wanted to ask what this episode and the class of the men had meant to her, but he'd never gotten around to it. He knew these events represented a conundrum that had no happy answers, no light he wanted shed on someone he loved.

Her immediate quandaries, on the other hand, made ready sense. Rosemary had expensive tastes and no income. Her children were hitting that angry and unforgiving phase. The joke was that he himself had advised her to find a rich man, not some guy who wanted to quit his job to paint landscapes. He had told her this in a tone of offhand objectivity, as if he himself were a pragmatic man of the world. Now, apparently, she was taking him at his word.

At that moment, some yards ahead of him down the orange shadows and hollow spaces of the mall, the figure of Rosemary's eldest daughter's boyfriend — a skinny, goateed kid whose nickname was Satan — went skittering around the corner as though he were being blown over the slick tile by a cold, subterranean wind. On the turn his long black hair swung like the lank string on a totem mask and the red tattoos quivered and burned against his lean white arms as he scrambled for balance. Nobody else was in view and the sight of this baleful kid made Arthur flinch, as if he'd seen a bat flitting through the concourse. There was a night last winter when Rosemary and Arthur were making love in her room: the sound of a male voice came through the wall and stopped him cold. "Who's that?" Arthur asked, looking up, catching his breath. It was two in the morning and the adjacent bedroom was shared by her daughters, sixteen and fourteen years old. Arthur couldn't believe that Rose was letting this kid spend the night with both girls, lying on the floor between their beds, talking at them for hours. Now that he thought of it, his own lovemaking with Rose had fallen off after that night.

He passed the corner and looked down toward the rows of telephones. The kid had disappeared and Arthur felt that this adolescent who called himself Satan had something to do with the present situation with Rose, something to do with her ultimate trouble. But the mall was empty and the black rain beaded down the glass doors he'd entered an hour ago.

He wandered into the bright cold supermarket, its upper reaches reminiscent of some vast hangar where secret aircraft are built. The night outside the long windows was dark and unknowable and he could easily imagine that this place did not exist, or that it had always existed, that it was where everything would be decided. Even now, down the mall, a critical drama of his own was unwinding whether he wanted it to or not.

He picked up a plastic yellow basket and plied the deserted aisles, dropping in a can of this, a package of that.

He had failed her. That much was now evident. She had offered him everything, the beauty of her person and the hellish crowded rooms of her past, everything held out proudly and foolishly for him to accept forever or defer to another man, another series of men, each one discovering her attentions like the first explorer to land on some lush continent whose contours matched precisely the shape of the fabulous place he had dreamed. He'd had his chance and without warning it had passed. Was that it? Was that what this night was about?

The supermarket was as empty as the mall, the few people here looked pale and zombie-like under the implacable artificial light. He was reaching for a jar of pickles when the lights flickered and the alarm went off, a loud jangling bell like a fire alarm in old movies. He looked up and down the aisle and saw no one. With the alarm sounding steadily he finished his shopping and made his way to the express counter.

The young woman snatched up each item the moment he placed it in front of her.

"Don't you love this?" she said, nodding toward the alarm that came from somewhere near the exit. "Doesn't this make your night?"

"What is it? What's going on?"

She swept the pickle jar over the scanner and tapped digits into her register. "A water pipe burst in The Dollar Store. It set off alarms all over the mall. Don't ask me. I don't understand the system."

She finished her tabulations while Arthur pushed his groceries into two plastic bags. The bell clanged urgently, but there didn't seem to be anyone around to hear it.

Drifting back toward the department store, either arm weighted with an overloaded bag, Arthur kept an eye peeled for Satan. Early last summer, when Rosemary first divulged the extremity of her situation, Arthur had feared the worst: threats, abductions, deaths that looked like accidents... "Don't worry," Rose had said, "they probably wouldn't bother with you." But in the end, if this was the end, the whole show had been brought down by a kid who called himself Satan. There had been real love here, but somehow the kid and the mall and the long indoor winter had blighted their hearts' best intentions.

The food courts were still vacant; the wide corridor that veered off to the telephones and rest rooms had an appearance of dim endlessness, as though it descended to the centre of the earth. The bells that had faded behind him were getting louder again as he approached the department store. He could see Rosemary and Jean and LaChance sitting around the table, the only humans in sight. He could barely hear Rosemary talking and he knew suddenly and certainly that his fears were on target. She was telling LaChance one of the exotic stories that revealed everything and nothing, that acted like a striptease or a highball for sheer stimulation but betrayed little of the bitter grist of her actual far-fetched life.

The seated three did not look up as he came closer. Muzak mixed with the alarm. It made Arthur think of revelations she had delivered in the car when his eye was on the road and his ear distracted by the friendly white noise of AM radio, an inane tune from the mid-sixties. The brightness of those tunes deflected the shock of her statement so that he listened and nodded and kept driving, his attention on the larger world like a kind of denial while the dread of her confession seeped into the cracks and corners of his distracted mind. It was as though her stories were dreams she had told him, and his ability to dream the same dream with her, to re-dream it with redemptive meaning, provided her with an identity she had never been able to forge for herself. This theory struck him as important and new and as he stepped back into the group he was desperate to get her alone and spill it, make her see that he had something to offer that would ultimately thwart bad fate; only he had the power to go back and alter the soul-crushing past because only he dared to imagine it in all its terrible implication and bewildering actuality. She was sitting there, flirting and appealing to a near-stranger — asking him, in effect, to save her life — and he, Arthur, had already gone into her hell and at least a part of him, he now realized, would dwell there forever.

The bells were still pounding someplace in the wall directly behind and above Rosemary. As he set his groceries on the metal chair beside the display table he heard her telling LaChance one of the stories that she'd told him at the beginning, an anecdote from her colourful girlhood in Malaysia. She seemed to finish or catch her breath and LaChance mentioned that he liked to hunt. Rosemary, flushed and pale at once, broke in to describe how her father had taught her to shoot a machine gun on the very day she was to be married.

"I was crazy with a million things and he drags me out to this range and makes me shoot this monstrosity at a target."

Her voice was strained, going rapid-fire to compete with the alarm, to match the machine gun she wanted LaChance to see in her hands.

"Imagine it," she said. "He keeps me out there until I can hit the target. On my wedding day!"

For the past year Arthur had followed that voice and its stories, picking up their charms, trying to attach them to that other history of devastation. Now both the golden and grotesque had been told once too often to signify anything other than her womanly desperation, and what remained was this harsher, hungrier voice that clashed with the unrelenting bells.

Arthur had stood there a full minute and nobody had acknowledged his return with so much as a glance. Jean shuffled some papers on the table. They were friends, and he expected some sign from her that she was hip to what was happening, but she gave none. LaChance sprawled in his chair and watched Rosemary talk, a conflicted grin on his neatly bearded face.

"My father made me shoot that gun," she said. "He also made me parachute out of a hot air balloon the day I turned sixteen."

Arthur knew some other things her father had done to her. He wondered when she would get around to telling LaChance about them.

He took a seat beside his groceries; only then did Rosemary stop to look at him.

"We thought you might not come back," she said.

"I came back. I always do."

She returned her attention to LaChance and plunged into another story, about an American pilot she dated in Germany while she was a teenager in boarding school. "He was very quiet, very sweet. He was killed over Vietnam."

She paused, her eyes downcast, briefly troubled by the memory of this other time. Then she started a different story about a different pilot, a black American soldier: the first man to teach her to slow dance. It was Halloween, 1966, she was just a kid, and then, touched by another Halloween memory, a darker one from her last marriage, she faltered again, momentarily overpowered by the darkness and the clangour of the bell which descended like a punishment: stroke after stroke beating down on Rosemary's erect shoulders in the diaphanous pastel dress. Had she been alone, had this been the ordinary Rose, she would have promptly fled the building to escape that sound. Now her face was bluish-white with two spots of rouge high on her pretty cheekbones; the fractured mouth, still lovely in its brokenness, was distended and working fish-like for air, hope, something she must have to survive. Even LaChance, Arthur figured, must see what was happening here. Even a salesman in a silk suit and shoes with tassels must see the desperation that clashed with stroke after stroke of the deafening alarm.

A jolt of silence made Rosemary catch her breath, look around. The bell had stopped. She pressed a hand to her exposed clavicle.

"Oh my God," she exclaimed, theatrically gasping, "have I been talking over that thing all this time?"

Arthur sat there watching, stunned, unable to lift an arm or leg. He stared at Rosemary, who felt his stare and said, "Oh dear, look at me, I must go to the ladies' and tidy my hair."

The way she pushed at her pinned hair with a slim, half-limp hand, the way she used that word "tidy" struck him as the mannerisms of some leading lady in a black and white film: a great tortured beauty on her final stand, unravelling seductively, flamboyantly, doomed yet appealing to all the worst instincts in the men around her. Doomed, but doing a suggestive dance before the ravening world. "Tidy my hair," she said, rising, jerking her slender arms, skating away on little self-conscious steps, her lavender heels clicking down the tile.

The other two sat without speaking, struck by the quiet which felt immense and unfathomable after Rosemary's voice and the violent alarm. Arthur had seen something in her walk that further confirmed his suspicion that she meant to snag LaChance. He sat there staring, dully aware that she had strewn her flamingo-bright stories by the other man who could not guess that there was a chink of terror between each and that together they produced a beauty almost unnatural and finally outside anything LaChance might have experienced in the arena of sex and romance. How could Arthur tell him or all the other men who would set eyes on her for the first time what he knew about her — that she collected china figurines of birds, that she had witnessed murder — and why hadn't he been able to question the rage which occasionally leapt out during lovemaking when she would curse and flail at him, then hold him fast and weep so copiously that his neck and chest would be slick with tears?

He looked up at Jean, wondering what she'd made of Rosemary's performance. Jean reached over to the chair between them, the chair that held his groceries, and moved both bags to the floor, as if their presence was queering the brisk professional aspect her exhibit required. As she lowered the bags LaChance tapped a pencil against his knee and glanced toward the corridor. In a moment Rosemary reappeared, smiling, her makeup reapplied, her hair prim and shining. For the first time Arthur noticed the white in it; not grey, but streaks of glittery white swept back from her temples into the dark coppery coil as though bleached by the very intensity of her thoughts and emotions.

Rosemary took her seat, smoothed her lap, and affected another long shudder, saying: "That goddamn bell made me feel like my head was coming off."

Jean rearranged some flyers on the table and looked around.

"I don't get it. This place is absolutely barren. Where did everybody go?"

Rosemary said, "Absolutely barren and Arthur is the only one who shows."

The muzak came down clearly from the ceiling. It was that ubiquitous tune from a Sixties movie, one that Arthur had heard in supermarkets and elevators most of his life, one that he and Rosemary had heard just last summer while they drove in the country and she told tale after tale about her adolescence and young womanhood abroad. In spite or because of the carefree inanity of that tune — redolent of harmless afternoons in stores and dentist offices and sunny strolls when she knew she looked as good as any woman in town — it somehow threaded those early chapters together with playfulness and glamour, a flavour of international fashion in the mid-sixties when her mind could cakewalk in a miniskirt and the world was her runway. The precarious grandeur of that lit his imagination: like Brigitte Bardot meeting the Beatles in some airport surrounded by crowds, waves of raw excitement, paparazzi. But it was Rosemary drawing the attention, Rosemary slowing cars and getting rings and mink coats from worldly strangers and honestly believing there were no strings attached... All of that and his own brief adventure with her, the silvery ether of his love and her hope going pop when she'd tell him about men she'd fucked in parks or at parties; her tearful, ecstatic admission, "I didn't even know his name!" Which owned up to the act but not the despair that produced it. He'd meant to ask Why? but let it drop, scared thoughtless, wanting to get back to the song.

His great mistake, he realized, had been in allowing himself to imagine her life.

LaChance stood and thrust his hands into his pockets, jingling the loose change. "I've got to get out of here. I haven't had supper yet."

This was angled toward Rose, an invitation for her to make a sign, to respond that she hadn't had her supper either and join him.

"Fifteen more minutes and I'm going to pack it in here," said Jean. "This is nowhere."

LaChance paced a few yards toward the department store and back again. He seemed to understand that Arthur, just by showing up, had skewed the signals between himself and Rose. He took off his jacket and flung it over his shoulder.

"What the hell," he said, a little testily. "I might as well go home."

He waited one more moment for a response from Rose. She

plucked at the mauve silk around her neck and scowled at the floor.

LaChance offered short goodnights and disappeared into the department store. The clerks in there were starting to turn off their cash registers and one young woman burst into giddy, relieved laughter.

"I think we've done our duty here," Jean said. "It's an off night."

"Off is an understatement," Rosemary added.

Rosemary and Arthur helped Jean box the United Way pamphlets; they folded chairs, then the table, and fit it into a large nylon sack. They hauled all this through the department store and out to her car in the parking lot. The night was mild and moonless; a soft rain continued to fall steadily, dampening their hands and faces. Rosemary hugged Jean and kissed her, more goodnights were exchanged, then Arthur followed Rosemary back into the mall. In her heels she clipped off a short yard ahead of him, her chin in the air. She seemed angry.

"What is it?" he said as they made their way back through the pots and appliances. A pair of clerks, well-dressed young women from cosmetics or lingerie upstairs, turned to stare admiringly at Rosemary. He tried to keep pace with her, the domestic wares shedding a muffled lustre in the lowered lights as though they were props to a sweeter drama that he and Rosemary would never know. He supposed that he had never believed they could live together, given what he knew of her past: he couldn't see her living with anyone for long, or happily, but now he felt an absurd urge to protest his devotion and worthiness as a partner. He had failed her on this score, and the thought of her appealing to other men as she had to him — telling her story, revealing her needs — filled him with panic. She should have warned him. Certainly she could have warned him before she turned away, jumped so desperately at the first man to come along. Couldn't she see the danger out there? On some level, for all her prodigal experience with men, she still didn't understand who they were in the dark. She still didn't see there was one card that should never be tabled.

"Rose," he said, "Rosemary, come on. Talk to me. Tell me what's going on."

She tugged an earring, never slowing. Without looking at him, she said, "I have a few groceries to pick up."

She clipped off toward the supermarket where he'd first heard the alarm. He followed because she was going away, going away, and the day after tomorrow he'd leave town and that would be that. Tonight they were in that intermediate zone where he might still muster enough will to touch her, to know her as Rose for one last hour, though he knew his own desperation would repel her now, and in the morning she would be gone. In two weeks he might phone her, but she would no longer be Rose. He knew this with a heavy certainty that was half experience of the world and half knowledge of the woman herself. The essential Rosemary, whose essence was ever-changing, had once told him: "I never go back. Once I'm through with a man I'm through."

It was all happening too fast. As he followed her through the aisles, as she lingered over the aromatic chill of the produce coolers, he knew it was shutting down and whatever he had to say or show her about Arthur and Rosemary must be said or demonstrated now. But that made it impossible. He picked up an orange and blinked at it with recognition and surprise: actual fruit in his actual hand, ripe for consumption. An entire world, and he had lost it.

He returned the orange to its bin and rushed after her, wanting to slow things down, to bring her back to the round, full moment like a celebration they could enter, that they could share like a fruit in the hand. He would peel it and pass it to her, and she would close her mouth on the sweetness and they would have that sweetness between them. Forever, but only now. That and nothing else was love, and they understood that, she and he.

She was at the express, chatting at the same woman who'd complained about the alarm.

"I know you from someplace," Rose told her. "What's the name?"

The woman touched the tag on her tunic: Elizabeth.

"I met you at the United Way picnic," the woman said.

"Right! Of course," chirped Rosemary, bagging her packages and cans. "A few of us from the office were set up at *The Bay* this evening." She chattered on as she gathered her plastic bags. She strode toward the exits, calling back, "Nice to see you, Liz!" And Arthur saw that she hadn't placed the woman at all, that she didn't even know that she didn't know the cashier in question.

"Wait for me," he said, bolting after her. "Wait a minute, Rose."

The automatic door had half shut, then swung wide again with a mechanical groan. She was standing under the entrance awning, her face tight, frowning as if she'd realized she had no idea where she was going.

"I'll drive you home," Arthur said. "I'm parked just out there."

She straightened and tucked her chin, staring out at the dark rain.

"All right," she said. "I'll wait here."

He understood that she expected him to bring the car around while she waited under the shelter. It was the sort of favour he'd seen his father and uncles perform for their wives, women who could never conceive of the life Rosemary had lived, all that sensation both exalted and profane.

He hunched off into the rain, wondering about the riot of sense experience she had known. He could almost see the sexual tilt of the streets she had seen on certain nights coming out of clubs with her husband, both of them coked and spinning toward further ecstasies of violation; he could see her frightened, hungry face and he could almost imagine the awful shock of that moment when she gave away her soul, the moment of terrible ecstasy and the immediate waning, those succeeding moments when an intolerable sadness descended and she knew that she was dying. Next morning she sat in her suburban garden, the heat coming down, and she knew she was dead; still lovely, still racked with appetite, but utterly dead in her soul. That's when her mouth cracked. That's when the song ended and a stillness of night and rain filled the empty room where her spirit had lived.

He unlocked the car door and stood there with his head bowed.

How did he know these things? How had she persuaded him to step into that empty room with his books and music and pictures, all the heart's small gifts that could not, finally, dispel the sadness of that place?

He could not forget one summer afternoon following hours with Rose in his bed. He'd rolled over, perfectly spent, and suddenly entered a waking dream, a clear prescient knowledge that Rosemary would appear to him on the instant that preceded his death. She'd stroll up to him with her panthery barefoot tread and exclaim, "Hello there, Rexino!" — her love name for him — and she would calm and comfort him and finally escort him into what came next. Hers would be the last human aspect before the film ran out. That afternoon as they lay in his bed he felt the certainty of his vision and threw his arms around her and felt the vivid strangeness of her, as if he'd just mated himself to the illusion of a woman who would soon turn back into a fish or gazelle.

He came back with the old Dodge, the engine mumbling. She stepped out of the shadows and he reached across and swung the door open.

Rose leaned toward the car and said, "I'll sit in back."

He stared at her through the dark. "What?" he said. "What are you talking about? Come on, get in."

"Well," she said, grimacing. Then she opened the back door, deposited her bags on the back seat, and slid in up front.

"It's an odd night," Arthur said, accelerating slowly through the mostly vacant lot.

They turned onto the road, the wipers swiping at the spring rain that misted the windshield. Arthur touched the brake before the speed bump. Her building was immediately around the corner, on the edge of the wide black parking lot. Up on the eighth floor her apartment lights cast a glow on the small balcony. One night they'd sat up talking for hours on that balcony, drinking wine, then coffee, the ghostly lights from the mall filtering through a humid wall of fog. Come summer she would have to move to someplace cheaper, and that would mean more change, another kind of ending. As he turned down the dark entrance road to her complex, Arthur felt that he was driving through the dark sea of her stories, the dense web of her narrative which defied daylight logic, yet in the warm spring night everything she had told him existed out there, everything touched everything, and her lies and obfuscations melted away under the meaning of that contact. He had been intrigued and baffled by the way her stories could change, the way terror turned to titillation — but always he was inclined to believe in the sweetness of the cinema in her head. Despite the fear and denial and nearly inconceivable abuse, he held dimly to some notion of grace that would grant her transcendence. Last winter while they were browsing through a used bookstore she picked up a volume of children's verse and sang the innocent lyrics in an airy English voice that brought tears to his eyes and business to a standstill as everyone turned to look.

The Dodge swung around the parked cars behind her building and slowed in front of the lit doors.

"Thank you for the ride, Arthur," she said. She made a move to get out and he reached for her hand.

"Wait," he said. "Rose, talk to me. What's going on? What was all that with LaChance tonight?"

"With Gordon?" she said. "Nothing. What do you mean? Nothing was going on."

She stared straight ahead. He could see her perfect silhouette against the rain-bleared reflections in the window.

"All right. Never mind. Never mind that. But Rose, why are you angry with me? Is it the trip? We've been over that. It's just a couple of weeks. We've talked about it."

"Of course," she said. "I understand exactly. Now I should go."

"Rose, please," he said.

He sat there breathing the perfume heightened by the rain on her hands and hair. He knew that when his car gave her up, when she shut the door and disappeared into the bright lobby with her grocery bags, the stories would begin to separate and drift like ice floes in the night. The gaps would widen. The inconsistencies would show. Her voice would fade.

"Wait," he said, "please wait," and he got out of the car and went behind it around to her side and opened the door.

"What?" she said, alarm in her eyes. "Arthur, I'm going now."

He crouched beside her and the open door, lower than Rose in the car, and laid his hands on her knee. "Please," he said. He could feel the silk of her dress and the moulding of her flesh beneath it. He went down on one knee and let his hands fall to her feet, turning and lifting them toward him.

"Arthur," she said.

He slid off her shoes and let them clatter softly to the wet asphalt.

"Don't go," he said. "Don't go. Not yet."

She looked down at him, sadly, half-surprised, shaking her head.

"Rosemary," he said, and he kissed her feet. One, then the other, high on the arch.

She stiffened, as if the kisses hurt. "Don't," she said. "Arthur, no."

He kissed them again. He kissed her painted toes through the stockings. He held her feet together and kissed their soles. She made a small effort to pull away, but he held her feet and kissed them again, and then again, in the dark and warm falling rain.

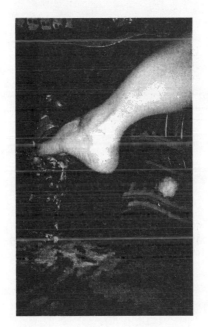

THE ART OF THE POSSIBLE

The hot weather was finally coming on, and Gerry's attention kept drifting to the open window behind the pale young woman in his office. He heard himself ask the standard questions and he heard the words that came from her mouth, but his mind moved from the words to the rare blue framed behind her and a telephone conversation he'd had thirty minutes earlier with Sharon. He'd caught her rushing to a meeting with some city councillors where she would pitch her case for increased funding. Sharon was the public library's chief administrator and she ran the system in an aggressive corporate mode. The building itself was sleek and new, with computers and VCRs and scanners and wheelchair ramps that looked like they could launch fighter jets, thanks to her competence and zeal. Gerry imagined rumpled politicians wilting before the brisk imperatives of her rhetoric, simultaneously intimidated by her intelligence and turned on by her three hundred dollar suit.

A small, summer-scented breeze entered the room and lifted a corner of the paper on his desk. The young woman before him — all of nineteen, mother of two, and abused by the man she'd been living with for six months — fell silent and watched him. Her face was tired and bored and thin, ready for the worst or nothing.

"What about your family?" Gerry asked. "Would your mother be willing to help with the kids now and then?"

The woman blinked and considered the question. Gerry knew she was trying to couch her answer in terms that would communicate some truth and retain an element of the respectable. Although this was their first meeting he knew the crux of her dilemma through and through. His job was to persuade her to come in from the cold, to reject the world she'd been born into and to join the one her older, more favoured sisters had created.

"Listen," he said, "it's time for you to think about yourself. It's time to think about your needs. There's no shame in that. You have the right."

She kept her pale blue eyes on him. What did she see? In her world, men like Gerry were not really men. Men who made a living by talk were laughable, beneath notice, like cartoon rabbits.

"But listen to me," he said. "You don't have to stay with him. There are options. There's no law that says you have to take it. In fact, the law says he can't treat you this way. There are options."

She was wan and freckled and unimpressed. A volley of pigeons flashed through the square of blue behind her, the sound of their wings like leather slapping leather.

He picked up his pen and put it down again.

What the moment needed, what the whole damned age demanded, was some levity. Some insouciance. Maybe he'd tell her about his conversation with Sharon, the story she'd hurried through on her way out... Last night, just before the library closed at seven, a plainclothes cop had nabbed the character who'd been defacing books for months, a sad and sick man who'd not only blotted out every reference to the Deity he came across in any book or magazine, but who also left his own ejaculate on their open pages. The best part was that the offender had tried to run for it: he'd made a dash for the exit and the cop had to tackle him and radio for backup. Just a tubby, middle-aged guy, Sharon said. A regular at the library. As they led him away he laughed hysterically and shouted, "I am the Lonely Bull!" and "Bring out the hermaphrodites!"

Gerry looked at the woman before him and decided he wouldn't tell that one. He rubbed his eyes and glanced again at the completed questionnaire on his desk.

"The first step," he said, "is to make up your mind to help yourself. That's what it takes to make progress."

She nodded and looked over her shoulder as if to see for herself what had been drawing his attention to the window. At the end of the interview he repeated his admonition and gave her some literature. He stood and shook her hand. The gesture seemed to perplex her, as though shaking a man's hand was something out of the ordinary. He could tell by the way she turned and shuffled, moving obliviously in shabby sneakers and an unnecessary pink ski jacket, that he probably wouldn't see her again.

After the door closed he sat behind his desk and stared at the sky outside and above him. The air and light that filled his office had nothing to do with human logic or the young woman's problems. The return of summer always struck him with his own irrelevance and the mitigated futility of his work. The long winter had been fraught with mental striving and circular talk; this winter, more than others, he had come up against the immensity of his task and the actual negativity of his effect. His basic message to the oppressed, he realized, was that things can only get worse, and usually do. So get out now.

In a nutshell, that was it. That was all he knew.

But summer had come just in time. It was his partly conscious hope that summer would save him from his own thoughts. Summer would save everyone. In a week or two the entire town would surrender its beliefs and disappointments to the inevitability of the season. The town would lay down its pride and politics and leave off trying. The new and unsignifying sun would render all that transparent and void. Just in time, the streets would be given back to them.

When the phone rang he looked at it for a long moment before lifting the receiver.

Walking home, along the heaved and broken streets dappled with paisley shadows and sunlight, between the green budding trees and old brick houses, Gerry congratulated himself for noting the changing necessities of time and place, for having a sense of himself and his vocation in history. Likewise, he considered that he might be losing his already qualified faith in social work. Times were changing. The meaning of the work was not static. He told himself that he was not unlike any professional of his acquaintance. Everyone he knew secretly despaired of the system; only the profoundly angry insisted on its efficacy and right. The new world of justice and equality was cracked because nobody believed the same things or the same way. The last five years at the counselling centre had been an education in this direction. The office had been established on the unlikely marriage of public funds and private endowments in the name of a well-known and wildly admired local feminist, a charismatic woman with a nearly religious following. When she died of cancer six years ago hundreds had filled a downtown theatre to pay tribute and share a high, delicious grief. The most curious part of the proceedings, to Gerry's mind, occurred when one of the deceased's associates, a large and fierce-looking woman with a brushcut, gripped the podium and declared, "I'm just thankful it was a brain tumour and not ovarian." Gerry had turned that sentence over in his mind for months. From time to time, when he was doing laundry or driving a long distance, he still thought of it. From time to time he reflected on the possibility that the two women who worked at the centre with him were clandestinely disapproving of his presence there, though plainly they did not view him as the enemy.

In this and most cases, he supposed, it was a question not of essence, but mode.

Last month he'd counselled an unhappy couple trying to find common ground. He sensed that they cared for each other, that they possessed a genuine rapport, but when he asked the woman if she loved the man she missed a beat, and then said, "No." The man stiffened and winced and Gerry realized how easily he'd set the poor guy up for a terrible denial. But the man rallied briefly and cried, "She didn't love me even when she loved me!" And Gerry understood that the man was trying to tell him that this woman, who reminded him slightly of Sharon, could not admit the existence of love or any belief in it even when that love was inside her, even when she held it for this particular man.

That was the problem. How to make any relationship work when nobody could agree on the meaning of the big feelings, the big occasions of the heart.

Turning the corner, he came face to face with the mayor, a bright and articulate woman who wore second-hand clothing and grim smiles. Sharon had known her in university, a fact that always struck Gerry as obscurely significant. Unlike Sharon, the mayor seemed to truly suffer in her work, as if saddened by the unrelenting dinginess of her colleagues and their daily concerns.

She spoke a clear greeting as they passed, and he wondered if she knew him — if she actually knew his name and station in the community, or just his face on the street.

And after all, who was he? Another fading hippie gone straight in khaki slacks and topsiders, another mental-health pro in a town choking with shrinks and lawyers. A single man with several Masters degrees and a genuine love for aerial photography. He was a middle-aged citizen, ultimately, with good intentions and waning ambition.

"Avoid the pressure of self-definition," he'd recently told a client. "On the other hand, get in touch with yourself."

He'd delivered these words without irony or self-consciousness. In retrospect, he supposed it was possible he was missing something. For instance, the woman in his office this afternoon. What had he offered her when you got right down to it? What was the substance of his expertise? Perhaps he'd see her again. Maybe she'd come back and get caught in the middle. Those were the tough cases, the ones caught between two worlds, between the context of their origins and the brave idea he offered them. They suffered most. They came and went and came again when things got bad. He had no choice but to witness the process. If they cracked up or their men cracked up, it came back to haunt him. He hated these cases partly because of their seeming ambivalence toward their own lives, and partly because he felt a shadowy culpability. If he couldn't persuade them, if they didn't come over, he had only guaranteed their misery by feeding it with wispy promises of a better life, a life they could barely imagine and most had no means to access.

He walked on, almost sleepily. On the next block he regarded the century-old edifice — replete with historical marker — which had been the birthplace of a celebrated national leader and more recently the habitation of a notorious pederast.

The world, Gerry decided, was full of wonder if you didn't think about it too much. That was the trick. Not to think too much.

His house was in the north end, on one of the better streets in a nearly respectable neighbourhood. He was surrounded by older retired couples and graduate students; on evenings like this, with the windows open and the soft air carrying dim laughter and baseball on the radio, he counted himself blessed. He lay on the couch and looked at his carpet and furniture, the antique floor lamp and the framed photographs on the wall. They were all comforting and comfortable. This weekend he'd drive out to the airfield and go up for an hour or so with Eddie Chang. Later, they'd have a beer on the patio of their favourite bar in town and talk cameras and flying. Who could complain? Thinking about these good things, Gerry fell asleep on the couch. An hour later he woke without surprise or chagrin and fixed supper in the clean, tiled kitchen.

At ten-fifteen, while he was watching the news, Sharon phoned. She called him every night at this time, because by then her daughter was in bed, and each night she seemed to think the regular and punctual contact somehow relieved her of actually visiting Gerry or inviting him to her place. None of this pleased him, but he had learned the futility of trying to push her; any word or gesture that resembled an intrusion of his will had an immediate and chilling effect on their relations. Over time he had decided that the nightly calls which linked their weekend liaisons were sufficient. At this point in his life, working a job rife with stress and depression, he wanted no waves. What he had with Sharon, what she allowed them, was good enough.

Tonight she was preoccupied with the day's events, that ugly business about the cops nabbing the man. Tonight her attitude was less whimsical. The affair made a great story, but it was troubling to contemplate.

"What would make a human being do something like that?" she asked. "Where in the world would a person get such an idea?"

"I don't know. He sounds more interesting than the folks we get at the office. I wouldn't mind his sort for a change."

Sharon made a sound of dismissal and said, "That's because most of your clients are women. It would never occur to a woman to leave her bodily fluids on an open book."

Gerry thought about this. He supposed it was true, and that there were several ways to look at its meaning.

"Anyhow," he said, "I wish somebody with a new problem would walk into my office. The library gets some bona fide cranks. We get the dull, serious trouble."

He heard Sharon put her hand over the receiver and speak

into the distance, followed by the soprano inquiries of her twelve-year-old daughter, Nicola. Through the phone and the wire and Sharon's capable, womanly hand, he heard her say, "No one, dear. Go back to bed. I'll tell you later."

He waited for Sharon to come back.

"I am the Lonely Bull," he said. "Bring out the hermaphrodites."

He thought he heard Sharon kiss her daughter, and then she coughed lightly, shifted the phone, and said, "Sorry about that."

"No problem."

"So what about the weekend, Gerry?"

He told her about Eddie Chang and the plane and suggested Sunday afternoon.

"Okay," she said. "But come a little later. Two or three."

"We'll be down by noon," he said, "but two is good."

They said goodnight and he hung the receiver on the wall. Had her tone been somewhat more formal than usual? Had he perceived an ever-so-slight reticence or anxiety between the lines?

He turned out the kitchen light and then killed the TV in the living room. No point in over-analyzing. He knew the dangers of that. Most likely, Sharon was worried, working too hard. All he had to do was give her no grief.

That was all she asked.

In the night he dreamed the phone rang and he answered it in the dark. The instant he put the receiver to his ear the voice began a black torrent of jeers and damning facts, facts about Gerry and Sharon and the rest of them, everyone who called the shots and set the pace in this town. The voice was clear and guttural, like the voice of an underworld malignancy, a misshapen demon, but then he recognized it as Tom Moriarty's, Sharon's alcoholic ex-husband, a man Gerry had met maybe twice, and then only in passing, several years ago. But this was certainly Tom, returned from the place he'd gone to after Sharon, sharing his bitter knowledge and experience in a voice of deathly knowing. In the dream Gerry was unable to hang up the phone; it was not in his power to break the connection, and instead he had to pull away from it by inches, retreating by a steady exertion of fear and will, until the voice receded in the dark and with one last thrust of panic, Gerry woke himself, blinking and breathing hard on his dishevelled bed.

He listened and got up and crossed the room to the window. He shifted the blinds and peered down at the potted asphalt and ragged lawns illumined by the streetlamp. After a while he went back to bed, but the voice of his dream stayed with him, and for a second he believed that Tom was dead, that this was the voice of a dead person imparting his hard-earned knowledge to the man who was closest to the woman who'd been his wife for fifteen years.

Gerry turned on the light and tried to clear his mind. The night was too short to squander on such thoughts. But what a voice. What an idea: Tom Moriarty come back after all this time with the authority of death. What had the voice in the dream actually said? Gerry couldn't remember the words, only the dark, frightening stream of bitter truth and deathly knowledge. What were they doing, anyway? He and Sharon and the mayor and the rest — what were they about? What was their work in the world? What were they doing swimming back and forth in the self-important present while that larger trouble came ever closer by deceptive degrees?

He switched off the light and lay back on his bed.

Everything was journalism, he decided. An exploitation of the heavy facts and portents. They were turning true events and happenings into a thin, literal grist for the machine. What he did in his office was a kind of emotional journalism, a technique for rendering horror and loss into a prose his clients could read back to themselves in the night. They both knew trouble was coming, but who could name it? Who could separate the sick fatigue in his or her heart from the dull encroachment of history?

He closed his eyes and tried to clear his head.

On the weekend he'd fly with Eddie Chang. Blue sky and a

lap full of maps and lenses, equipment he'd purchased with long hours and careful budgeting. Later he'd see Sharon and they'd barbecue chicken in her backyard. When Nicola was in bed Sharon would lead him into the den and they'd take off their clothes and make love on the floor. And Tom Moriarty would not be present. When they did it on the floor, Sharon's lost husband would not exist.

It was almost two o'clock when Gerry parked in front of Sharon's house on Sunday. The morning had been perfectly blue and serene, and before he turned the key he sat behind the wheel for a minute longer to listen to the radio. The song it played was a favourite oldie, one he hadn't heard in ages, a song that reminded him of all the perfect Sundays in his life. He sang along and tapped the wheel and when he got out he breathed deeply of the sweet June air, a rush of green and flowering humidity.

He walked around to the backyard and lingered at the descending stone steps. Sharon was working over a plot of broken earth. He stood there and admired her: a comely middle-aged woman in loose mauve shorts and a man's undershirt with thin shoulder straps that exposed her brown shoulders and a soft flash of swaying breasts. She wore her daughter's baseball cap and tortoise-shell sunglasses. Gerry admired the substance of her shoulders and the neat fall of metallic red hair around her face. Standing there, just down from the sky, he felt lucky and alive, and smart — like a man who has made the right decisions, someone who knows what counts.

Sharon stood and stretched and looked around at him.

"Gerry, you move like a ghost."

"I don't feel like one. Just the opposite," he said. He started down the steps and she returned to her crouch over the soil.

"I just need to get these in," she said. "Just give me a minute to finish."

He sat on the low stone wall and watched her. The stone was warm and the sun fell hot and flatly on the yard. It glanced off the green beer bottle that sat on the wall a few feet to his right. He noticed it because of the tiny green fireball the sun made in the glass, and because he knew that beer wasn't Sharon's drink.

She stood up again and dropped her trowel. She gave Gerry a long, enigmatic regard through her expensive sunglasses.

"How was your morning?" she asked. "How is Eddie?"

"Eddie's fine. Morning was fine. What's that look?"

She grimaced slightly and wiped her hands on her hips.

"What's going on?" Gerry said.

"Let's take a walk," she said. "Do you mind? Can we just take a walk down the hill!"

He pushed off the stone ledge and took his own sunglasses from his shirt pocket. They were green aviators, the same green as the imported beer bottle beside him.

"Sure. Let's go."

They walked out to the road and started down the long hill. They passed a large white-columned house where an older couple in sun hats and Bermudas planted geraniums along their sidewalk. Sharon called hello and they glanced up quizzically and smiled. Gerry could see that they liked her as a person and appreciated her as a neighbour. He could see the order she had accomplished in her life, the urgency and solidity of her job balanced with an attractive domesticity. Good neighbours and handsome yards. Technically, this was not suburbia, but the ordering impulse was thoroughly suburban: the order of *You tend your garden and I'll tend mine.*

As he walked and listened to her cheery, mundane greetings, he realized a slow, black rage rising in his throat. Something was coming, something bad, and the pleasantness of this domestic landscape could only make it worse.

Relax, he told himself. Take it slow. Wait and see.

"Where's Nicola?" he asked.

"Upstairs playing computer games. That's all she does any more, lie around with her Game Boy."

Gerry remembered he'd brought a book about photography he meant to give Nicola. He'd been driving around with it in his back seat for days. When he mentioned this, the corners of Sharon's mouth twitched unhappily.

"What's the deal?" he said. "What's wrong?"

"Gerry, I have a feeling about the way things are going."

He walked beside her and waited. Then he said, "What feeling? What things?"

She drew an impatient breath, as if he were making her talk in a manner she found distasteful, as if he'd raised the topic in the first place.

"My life," she said. "I want my life back. We've been going on like this for months, and now I'd like my life back."

"Your life?" he said. He turned the words around in his head and tried to think what she meant. "Your life," he said. He felt the surge of anger and checked it. In his best professional tone, he said, "What are you saying? I meet you for lunch or drinks maybe twice a week, we actually clinch with no greater frequency, and you're telling me you want your life back. What does that mean?"

She walked on, her jaw set, but a kind of bleakness breaking behind her dark glasses.

"I mean," he said, "do you really think I have your life to give back? Do you think you've given me that much of it?"

"Maybe it's in my head," she said.

"That might be it."

"No. I mean maybe there's so much of you in my brain that I can't think of my real life. You take up too much space in my head and I can't remember what I'm really about."

"Is that possible?" he said. And then: "I don't believe it."

"It's true. I worry about you."

For a moment what she said struck him as almost wonderful. Then he understood that she didn't worry about him, she worried around him; he caused her a specific anxiety because she couldn't fit him into the general meaning of her life.

"I'm at an age where it's important to do the right things, to be pointed in the right direction. You know that, Gerry."

They reached the bottom of the hill where the paved road faded into ruts that trailed through green brush and meadow toward the highway. Standing there, he could hear Sunday traffic in the warm June wind, the sound of coming and going in the summer. Had he been at his desk on a winter afternoon he might have talked his way out of this. Within the context of his office and its rational mode he might have made her see that her worry was groundless, that he, Gerry, had no desire or need to consume her time or thoughts, that they might indeed go along as they had been, giving and taking in an adult manner without guilt or over-expectation. Guilt and high expectations were the root of most trouble with educated people. Surely she knew this. And consider the options. Compare her formless anxiety with the despair and actual danger faced by the battered souls who came to him daily — the women who knew they were bound to their feckless men; the men who knew they were absolutely screwed to their tin destinies. Compare your more-or-less pampered lot to theirs, and give me a goddamned break...

He emptied his chest and calmed himself. Like the majority of his clients he understood that his best chance was to surf the inertia.

"All right," he said. "Obviously you've given this some thought."

"I have," she said.

"All right. All right, then. Don't worry. We can do whatever you want."

She slowed and turned her face toward him and said, "Thank you, Gerry."

There was not much emotion in her voice and the bleak light around her glasses had solidified into something bland and relieved.

"It's all right," he said.

"Let's go a little further. Just a little, then we'll turn back."

They waded into the tall grass and weeds from the narrow dirt lanes. A rich, pollinated heat swam up through the green. He watched Sharon walk, just ahead of him, the sun reflecting on her fiercely red hair. He had no idea what she was thinking. If he had to, he couldn't say what had just passed between them or what came next. Nevertheless, he had the sense that something would come. He accepted what she had told him, but he felt that this was not the end. Not yet.

He said, "Don't worry, Sharon."

"I'm not," she said.

They moved through the field without speaking, Sharon just ahead. They climbed a small ridge and then went down into a grove of wild, stunted apple trees. In the warm, hidden shadows she let Gerry take her hand. They regarded each other through their dark glasses and Gerry had the sudden insight that this was what it was all about, this facelessness and blessed relief from personality, this was what the world was coming to. Here in the trees, with her eyes hidden from his and his unknown to hers, there was the thrilling and necessary absence that she craved, that the world was moving toward.

He felt excited and calm at once, as though he were in the flux of some crucial but controlled experiment.

"Let's lie down," he said. "Let's just lie down here and forget the rest."

A brief, rueful smile flashed beneath the glasses, then her face went blank and she complied in a way that indicated she was feeling exactly the same thing. Though neither could name what this was, for once he felt certain that they were feeling exactly the same thing.

"Come on," he said, and he lay back on the grass and earth.

She knelt beside him and unbuttoned his shirt and unbuckled his belt. She pulled the belt free of his khakis with a long, slithery motion and flung it into the brush like a dead snake. She removed his shoes and then everything else except his sunglasses and manoeuvred herself over him so that she filled the bright quadrant of sky at the treetops and her tanned, static face looked down at him through her dark glasses and it was like being mounted by an alien or a god or a beautiful insect. She fitted him through the baggy pantleg of her shorts and began to ride him with heavy purpose, all the while looking down, abstracted, straight-faced, powerfully strange. She rode him harder, her breath rasping, her face still distant and other and the world he beheld through his glasses bore down on him like a current of green flame. He heard the faraway traffic on the hot wind streaming through the trees; he saw her tilt backward and watch him naked and eyeless below her. And though her expression was utterly detached, he felt her excitement pin him to the earth. High above them, a single-engine airplane buzzed slowly across the inverted bowl that held these fields and trees and Sharon's neighbourhood. Gerry imagined a high-powered camera in that plane, trained down on their conjoined form. He imagined the figure they made, an ultimate pictograph like those birds and beasts visible from the air over the bluffs and plateaus of Peru — symbols of extinct cultures that perhaps contained the key to their extinction. From the sky, it all made mysterious sense. She rose above him and her bluntly cut hair touched her square shoulders and suddenly she looked exactly like a sphinx; when he tried to speak she bent closer and her hair fell around her face and her breasts swayed beneath the thin undershirt and Gerry's excitement matched her own. For once, just this once, they were perfectly matched in the moment. He knew they were together inside that moment, and he let it happen. He watched it and wanted it and he let it happen.

When they were finished Sharon lifted herself and walked a few yards to the grassy incline that opened to a splash of sunshine beyond the trees. She waited there while Gerry reached for his clothing, and she seemed not to notice when he staggered getting into his pants. He stood behind her and for a long moment they listened to the wind in the trees. Gerry's knees had gone rubbery but his heart beat slowly, and if he had particular thoughts about what had happened he couldn't explain them to himself. He and Sharon started back through the bush and meadow, walking steadily and silently, side by side.

At the house Nicola was waiting on the porch. She sat sideways in a lawn chair and wore a long, discoloured T-shirt that stretched to her hips; her bare legs dangled over an arm rest. Pale and freckled and surly, as if she'd just climbed out of bed, she raised her face accusingly toward her mother and asked where she'd been.

"Gerry and I took a walk," Sharon said. She stood by the screen door to the kitchen and she seemed to stare toward the street.

"Why?" Nicola asked.

"Why? We wanted to talk, that's why."

Gerry lingered on the top step and leaned on the railing. For the first time that afternoon he took off his sunglasses. He realized that he had no idea what the hour might be or how long he'd been out there with Sharon.

"Well, Gerry," she said. She opened the door and turned toward him. "Thanks for coming over."

Her voice was even and slow; he could see Nicola's sprawl reflected in Sharon's glasses. It seemed to him that her words and voice had always contained this measured absence, this shapely void, and he felt stupid for not hearing it before.

He stepped off the stairs and crossed the lawn toward his car. As he unlocked the door his eye fell on the photography book he'd intended to give Nicola.

He stood beside the car, holding the book, looking at Sharon's house. Then he crossed quickly back to the porch. Sharon was gone and Nicola was just disappearing into the kitchen as he jogged up the steps.

"Here," Gerry said, but she had turned her back to him. "Nicola, here," and he held the book toward the closing screen door as the girl became a shadow behind it and the second door, heavy and windowless, shut with a distinct click that sounded like an inevitable word spoken by the house itself.

A Night in Tunisia

Bremmer was driving home from a barbecue at his thera-pist's house. In fact, he hadn't had a real session with the man in months because they'd become too friendly to maintain a professional relationship. Bremmer didn't mind. He was flattered that his therapist preferred him as a friend. Anyhow, he was mostly over the Eleanor business. "There are no endings, happy or otherwise," his therapist had said. "The only closure to be had is in finding something new. That's all there is." At last Bremmer had come to believe him, and even tonight, standing with a burger in his hand in a yard full of therapists — all of them ten years older than himself, Eleanor's age — he'd met a great woman who had lived in the same apartment he had five years ago. They figured she'd been there a tenant or two before Bremmer and he recollect-ed the place happily for ten or fifteen minutes. Someone asked him if he'd brought his trumpet; he said yes and maybe he'd play something later. But as the afternoon mellowed toward evening he felt himself drifting away; the house and the people in their bright summer clothes seemed to come through a filter of memory or dream. Their voices seemed to reach him across a calm summer lake, and he had that sense of being a ghostly scientist observing a pattern he could not enter. After tossing the frisbee a few times with his host, Bremmer said his goodnights and thank-yous and walked out to his car.

He drove down a country highway with the radio off and the windows open. The fields were green and roadside trees were gathering the stillness of early evening. As he drove he watched the fluid black shadow of his car ripple over the earth and he thought that summer was passing without any particular event or happiness to mark it, nothing at all to hook the season to memory.

Just before the turn-off to Eleanor's house he touched the brake and signalled. He had a job with the band tonight, but he felt no surprise or chagrin as he swung the wheel and climbed the hill through this town of leafy maples and disparate houses — impoverished locals beside affluent professionals who worked in the city. Eleanor lived alone in a restored farm house at the top of the hill, and as it came into view, serene beneath an emerging moon, he felt that surge of familiarity, as if this were his house and his town in the pleasant evening. The moon was exactly the moon he remembered, mysterious but domestic, warm but cool, the very fullness of the season hovering in its chosen spot.

Bremmer parked across and just down the street from her house, where he'd always parked, taking it in: all the good things that he'd been denied or that he had foolishly squandered. The scene was both sweetness and conundrum: his regard was part quizzical, part longing. He couldn't see Eleanor's car, but there was a brown Volvo in her driveway and he reckoned it belonged to Harvey McGoonan, the guy who'd phoned him out of the blue to accuse him of snapping off his car's antenna. Though he'd never met Harvey — a tall, hortative Scot with black beard and ponytail — he'd seen him with Eleanor in town, heard the overloud Scottish voice making its pronouncements in the open market on the square as he dickered over used books or picture frames.

"A man's automobile is his pride and function," Harvey had shouted over the wire. "The car is an extension of my property and domicile!"

Surprised, Bremmer laughed and told him that he was mistaken about the antenna.

In a rage, Harvey cried, "I cannot be mistaken! It's a *new car*!"

Bremmer laughed again and hung up, but he hated the extravagant brogue and its attitude of privilege: he knew Harvey taught Spanish at the university, that he was active and outspoken in leftist causes and occasionally quoted in the newspaper in relation to the latest regime in Guatemala or El Salvador. It was hard to match the voice on the phone with the man's press, hard to figure how a Volvo antenna would motivate him to dial up a stranger in wrath.

The moon was round and wide, bathing the street in soft clarity. He watched the sky for a while and started to pull away. Something about the house caused him to slow down again. He tried to see it as a disinterested neighbour might. Eleanor, a fortyish high school teacher living in a stolid, century-old house, had always been anxious about the eye of the community on her comings and goings, particularly the comings and goings of her men. She decried the city where she worked and despised the suburbs where her students lived, but her relation to this hybrid place was based on cool affability and prim indirection, a sublimated sense of her own superiority. Nothing was good enough for her. This was the best the world had to offer, but she must act as if none of it were enough.

He braked with both hands on the wheel. These were old, unhappy thoughts that made Bremmer feel low and not brave. He filled his lungs with the evening air and held it — the air from the neighbours' trees and Eleanor's garden. The same air she breathed in her sleep through the open windows upstairs. In a moment he'd let it go and drive home and the summer would be over. It was mid-July, but the season would be finished.

The thing about the house was that he had known it so intimately. He had allowed his affections, his loving imagination, to settle on its fronts and interiors. He had hung the storm windows and painted the frames on the old screens. He knew the bedrooms and bathrooms, the spacious downstairs with its chamber music and woodstove. And the upstairs study with its oversized paintings and the little fish that swam endlessly on the blue computer screen while they made love on the sheepskin Eleanor had flung to the hardwood floor.

Bremmer released the seat-belt; as he got out of the car he glanced at the boxy instrument case, drab and funereal, resting on the worn plush of the back seat. He pocketed the keys and crossed the pavement. At the foot of the sloping driveway he paused and listened, his attention drifting up and down the street, around the houses and trees that seemed to respire languidly in the lush July evening. For an instant the lemon-grey light tilted and stretched like a membrane that contained the real place, not past but hovering at a chimerical slant, and it occurred to him that if he entered at the proper angle it was still there, the whole world he loved, and his role in it. Still there, not behind him, but just to one side, as it always had been.

He walked up the gravel driveway and down the four stone steps into the backyard, a green oval of lawn and flower garden hidden from the neighbours and protected from the street by a tall hedge and a row of poplars. Bremmer looked at the ornamental pond Eleanor had dug and set with her own hands; his gaze fell on two empty lawn chairs arranged side by side and directed to take in the setting sun. He imagined Harvey and Eleanor in those chairs, speaking in easy, satisfied voices, sipping at glasses of wine. He felt, suddenly, the complete idiocy of his presence here. Also the danger. He cursed himself for succumbing to dinner with Eleanor last week. She'd met him only because Harvey was out of the country, and although she wanted Bremmer to know that she'd entered a new phase, she was temperamentally incapable of closure. Only fools burned their bridges, she maintained. And last week, over candlelight and calamari, she'd described her relationship to Harvey in neutral and nearly slighting terms. She said she really didn't know him that well, that time would tell how they got on. It sounded like something she was telling everyone who wondered if she wasn't falling too fast and hard. But Bremmer had wanted to believe in her indifference.

He shook his head and turned abruptly. As he climbed the stone steps he saw two figures enter the driveway, welling up in the twilight. Bremmer had the notion that they could not see him, that if he looked beyond them and proceeded without comment he'd pass unnoticed to one side or between them. If he held his concentration he'd slip between them like a wisp of ether or the fading chorus of a song.

The man straightened, released the woman's hand.

"Hold it right there," he said. "Kindly state your business."

The voice jarred with the quality of the evening. Bremmer made himself focus on the figures before him. They were tall and square-shouldered, and he saw how they made a couple. Eleanor had liked to remind Bremmer that she was a good two inches taller, and when he accused her of thinking like some kind of Aryan queen who demanded a perfect bodily match, she laughed and said, "Oh come on, that's what everyone wants."

He looked from the black-bearded man to Eleanor: she stood behind Harvey, faltering, and Bremmer realized she wasn't going to identify him.

"I came to see Eleanor," he said. "Eleanor knows me."

Silence held them in perfect opposition, until Eleanor

giggled — a strange and malefic sound in the gentle dusk of her yard. She raised her hand to her mouth and said, "Excuse me."

Harvey glared at her briefly. In the vagueness of the hour he looked like something Bremmer had always known he'd come up against someday. A solid tree in front of his skidding car; a renegade bear on the hiking trail. Any dumb but inevitable impediment that would alter his course and meaning.

"Look," said Bremmer, "I just came to see Eleanor. I thought she might be working down in the garden."

Harvey grimaced. The black beard sprouted wolfishly high on his cheekbones, making his face a long, vindictive V. He took a step closer to Bremmer and peered. The small, close-set eyes seemed to glitter out of a black thicket.

In a convoluted, Scottish accent he said, "I'm concerned about your purpose in coming here, chum, so I'm going to ask you to have your say, state your case, and then I want you to leave the premises. Understand? State your purpose here, and then you'd better move along."

The way he said "purpose" — so it sounded like porpoise — struck Bremmer with a feeling of sickly horror. How could Eleanor do it? How could she get close to a voice like that?

Harvey bowed his head and waited. Bremmer noticed that he was wearing a belt of purple hemp, and oily-looking sandals.

"All right then, wait a minute," Harvey said. "I don't know you. You don't know me. That's no reason not to behave like adults here. We surprised each other, right? I know how you must feel, seeing me and Eleanor together like this."

Bremmer looked at the house in which he had conducted his love with Eleanor. He remembered the big clawfoot tub in the chilly downstairs bathroom and the leak in the ceiling above the sink. He remembered crawling into the storage space behind the sofa in the den, the intimate darkness at the core of the house. These dimensions were as near and known as particular books Eleanor kept in her bedroom — the latest from Germaine Greer and a large glossy guide to glamour by Britt Eckland, an actress he barely remembered from the sixties. He wondered if Harvey knew them as he had, if he had simply replaced Bremmer as the eyes that took them in, or if the old facts of her life had been torn out and done over to compliment her new life with a new man.

"We should be mates," Harvey said, his enthusiasm growing. "Why not? We're all on the same side. Look," he said, pointing at Bremmer's chest, "that's a great shirt you're wearing!" The T-shirt featured a sharp black and white image of Dizzy Gillespie as a young hipster in hornrims and beret, smiling impishly and hugging his trumpet as though it were a trophy cup he'd just been handed.

Harvey said, "I love Diz! Dizzy is gr-r-rcat! We should be sitting inside drinking wine and playing his music."

Eleanor's cat materialized from under the porch and slanted wraith-like between Bremmer's ankles, arching familiarly and purring when he reached down to stroke its smoke-coloured coat.

Harvey extended his large, pale hand and, in a voice that declared and demanded goodwill, he said, "There's no reason we can't be mates, the three of us."

The cat vanished into the coming darkness and Bremmer stared after it, his mind blanked, his body unaccountably fatigued. What was he doing here? Why had he set himself up to endure the solicitations of this hirsute stranger in the place that had been his love and his home? How had this awful voice and overwrought ponytail arrived in his path?

"We're all on the same side, aren't we? Aren't we working for the same things?"

Bremmer blinked and looked at the outstretched hand.

"What?" Harvey said. "You refuse me?"

Bremmer turned to Eleanor. "Where'd you find this guy? What happened to all that psychic independence and integrity you've been talking about?"

Grey and indistinct behind the other man, she said, "I'm no part of this. None of this concerns me."

Harvey leaned forward and Bremmer inhaled the hot,

winey breath and looked into the small black eyes set too close beneath the prominent forehead.

"The truth is," Harvey said, his voice breaking, "Eleanor wants never to see you again."

Bremmer smiled. "That's not what she told me last week at dinner."

For a series of visceral instants this information travelled through Harvey and lit up his corners: the black scalp tightened, the tiny eyes sparkled; Bremmer perceived a distinct ripple of nerves along Harvey's jaw and then the inimical black eyes went dull, as if he'd stemmed the reaction by an enormous effort of will.

He gazed at the street and said, "I'll give you five minutes alone with Eleanor. Five minutes." He touched Eleanor's shoulder and withdrew down the driveway, into the street.

When he was out of sight, Bremmer said, "Christ, of all the crazies to hitch up with. Why that guy? Why him?"

Eleanor said, "You'd hate whoever I found."

"What? But this guy — I mean, that voice! He wears a ponytail for Christ's sake!"

"You drove me to him."

Bremmer stared. It had always been like this. When it came to Eleanor, his worst fears always came to pass. And none of it was her doing. It was a trick and a trap, but he knew what she meant.

"Besides," she said, "I can't believe you told him about last week. How can I ever trust you again? I should have known."

He stared at her grey and distracted face, her arms in silver-grey silk which she pressed to herself like a shroud.

"But it happened. Why shouldn't I say it? You were there."

She gave her head a bitter shake and said, "That's been our trouble all along. You always make it mean something. It always means something to you. I just can't believe you told him. Now nothing is possible between you and me. It's obvious. Now nothing is possible."

He felt his emptied mind turn over like a beached manatee,

some obscure sea mammal that had failed to find its element and outlived its function. He closed his eyes and tried to imagine the time when he had spoken her language and carried the key that had let him inside.

A car passed and from the trees a robin sounded a single, startled chirrup. When he turned again Harvey was there, his arm around Eleanor. The bravado was back in his voice and he asked her if she was all right, if everything was okay. Bremmer could hardly believe how she allowed him to play the man, to act out the role of rescuer and strong shoulder. He couldn't believe the way she seemed to need this from him, even as her pride despised it.

"I understand your feelings," Harvey said to Bremmer, "seeing us like this."

Eleanor held herself straight and noncommittal, eyes averted.

"I know you're hurting big time, chum. But you don't know how it is with Eleanor and me. We've just spent four wonderful days together. Four days and four wonderful nights. And I know how it must affect you, seeing us together."

Bremmer felt himself slump.

Harvey shifted toward Bremmer and settled his large hand on Bremmer's shoulder.

"I've been where you are now," Harvey said. "I've known those big, bad feelings. Don't worry, my friend, you'll come around. Be patient. Something else is out there for you."

The other man's voice was assured and burry, and Bremmer felt himself disappearing into it. His spirit deserted him there on the mowed grass beside the soft glow of Eleanor's house, and part of him had gone or was going toward that place where Eleanor did not exist. The voice and the heavy hand on his shoulder were urging him toward that place.

He started down the driveway.

Behind him, Harvey said, "If you ever want to talk, if you need someone to talk to, you can call me. I want you to know that."

Bremmer reached the street and started up the hill. He walked toward his car without looking back. But with his key in the door he stood and felt the full moon that engulfed the trees and filled the yards; he felt the intimate warmth of the street and once more the blue-cream front of Eleanor's house struck him as the very face of his last hope.

He stared at the house and tried to remember what had just happened. He looked at the house and felt the wide, warm moon shining on his brain. The phrase "four wonderful nights" went through his head in Harvey's voice. A faint shadow followed him as he retraced his steps down the hill and up the driveway. For a moment he lingered at the entrance to the yard. He saw them down in the garden, sitting on the picnic table, obscurely together in the moonlight. As he approached them he made out Harvey hunched upon the table top and Eleanor on the bench seat below, enclosed in his arms. Their faces were abstracted and void; it wasn't until he stood before them that Harvey turned his head.

"You said you'd talk anytime," Bremmer said. "Well, let's talk."

Harvey's eyes lifted as if he heard a dim voice but perceived no human form.

"What were you talking about?" Bremmer said. "Who were you kidding? You don't want to know me. You want me gone, that's all."

Eleanor sat in Harvey's embrace with her eyes downcast. They hadn't really noticed his return. They heard his voice, but they were miles away, deep in each other.

Bremmer said, "Face it. We're opposites, Harvey. We're opposites and there is nothing good between us."

Harvey glowered vacantly into the distance.

"Hey," Bremmer said, and as if to punctuate his previous thought and wake them to his presence he swiped lightly at Harvey's ankle with the rubber toe of his sneaker. Like a shot, the other man was on his feet. He pushed Bremmer backward and shouted: "Eleanor, call the police!"

Eleanor sat grey and horrified at the table.

"Eleanor! Do as I say! Phone 911!"

She rose and fled toward the house.

"For Christ's sake," Bremmer said, steadying himself. "Look, I'm going. All right? I'm going now. I'll just —"

Harvey jumped in his path and butted him backward with his chest.

"You're going nowhere until the police arrive!"

Bremmer started toward the street and Harvey cut him off again, bumping him with his chest. Harvey's jaw jutted doggedly and his eyes seemed to lock on the line of trees ridging the garden behind Bremmer.

He folded his arms and said, "I'm placing you under citizen's arrest."

Bremmer laughed and scowled. He made a couple of quick moves toward the street, each one blocked as Harvey sprang in front of him with a long, goosey stride, his arms folded to his chest — a sort of cartoon Highland dance that took them closer to Eleanor's porch.

Bremmer caught his breath and pushed the heel of his hand to his forehead. Lights were on in the house and he called out, "Eleanor, will you come here and clue this guy? Eleanor?"

Weaving and feinting, Harvey drifted between him and the street.

"Oh, for Christ's sake," Bremmer said and he took the porch steps in two bounds; the door was open. Inside, he was stopped by the actuality of the place, the fact that this was the kitchen where he had known Eleanor. He heard Harvey thunder up the steps, bellowing her name, but what Bremmer noticed was the new blue paint on the cupboards and the old varnish stripped off the table. He noticed the installation of copper pots and pans over the counter and the green shoots of certain exotic plants on the windowsills.

Harvey crashed through the door, shouting, "Look out! He's inside!"

He braked and straightened, tall and astonished that Bremmer had felt free to enter Eleanor's home, which already he must regard as an extension of his own. For an instant they faced each other. The tiny eyes held Bremmer on the

other side of the kitchen. Then Harvey edged forward as if
Bremmer were an escaped animal, a big cat that had slipped into
human surroundings by sheer boldness and cunning. The sweat
on Harvey's high white brow shone under the kitchen light; the
taut scalp twitched like a tight black skull cap. His hands hovered above his waist like a goalie waiting to block a shot.

"What's the matter with you?" Bremmer said. "Why do you
have to be the hero? I'll tell you something. Eleanor goes for
men with high causes and righteous energy. It's a turn-on. But
it doesn't really mean anything. Behind your back she's
laughing at you for caring in the first place."

Harvey advanced, backing him steadily into the adjoining
dining room.

"Eleanor!" Harvey screamed. "Where the hell are you? Did
you call them?"

Bremmer heard a creak in the hallway behind him and
both men looked. They knew she was there, they sensed her
tentative presence, but she didn't appear. Then, as though
she were speaking through the ceiling and walls from the
spirit world, they heard her flat and inflectionless voice:
"They're coming. I called them." Bremmer recollected her
earlier strained giggle, the involuntary snigger, and he wondered at the distance they'd come in an hour or so, from
being caught out in a crude triangle to phoning the police.
He also sensed that Harvey had been waiting for this. Weeks
or months ago he'd heard Bremmer's name, heard the reports,
and had silently determined to raise the stakes the moment
Bremmer entered the picture.

"All right, then," Bremmer said. "What's next?"

Harvey stood in the doorway between the dining room and
the kitchen, as if to prevent any escape. He lifted his chin
and said, "Now we wait for the police."

Bremmer smiled. "Come off it. Even the cops must know
the difference between criminal and heartbroken."

He caught Harvey's expression and hesitated. The black,
closely set eyes seemed to cross in cold fury.

"You are pathetic!" Harvey cried, his shoulders twitching.

Bremmer backed away and settled in the loveseat that faced the doorway to the kitchen.

Harvey glared at the wall a few feet to the left and above Bremmer's head. In a lower voice, he said, "Eleanor, where are you?"

She appeared silently from the hallway and stationed herself against the wall near Bremmer. He saw her as a shapely grey cloud; she seemed not to notice that she'd positioned herself on his side of the room.

"Well," Harvey said. "Are they coming?"

Her face was dazed, static. An expression that spoke everything and nothing in its refusal to signify.

Bremmer leaned forward in the loveseat and touched her arm.

"Eleanor, I know you don't want this. I know you don't want any police."

She blinked and drew her arm away. "This is difficult for me," she said.

Across the room Harvey watched everything. Bremmer's appeal to her had surprised him, in the same way that slipping into the house had caught him off-guard.

Bremmer stood and drew a breath.

"I need a glass of water."

Harvey focused and remembered himself. "Stay where you are!" He assumed an action stance in the doorway. "Sit down! You're not going anywhere."

Bremmer looked to Eleanor. "Hey," he said. "This is me. This is Bremmer. I'm just asking for some water."

She wouldn't meet his eye.

Harvey held his position in the doorway as though he expected Bremmer to make a break for it.

"All right," Bremmer said. He shrugged and resumed his seat. "So much for the brotherhood of Dizzy Gillespie."

Harvey straightened as if he'd been slapped. The bad blood filled the veins in his neck and around his eyes. His scalp tightened in another wave of rage and he took two strides into the room and raised himself on tiptoe over the loveseat.

"You know nothing about the music of Dizzy Gillespie!"

Eleanor blanched and faded into the hallway, a grey ghost withdrawing into its own grey space.

Bremmer sensed that if he so much as touched this man they would have genuine tragedy on their hands. Still, he had the urge. He wanted to pull that ponytail. Or maybe if he released the tight elastic Harvey would relax and let him go. Maybe all that rage was the result of poor blood flow.

"Where are those fucking police?" Harvey shouted. "We could all be dead ten times by now."

He lifted the receiver on the wall and punched buttons as though it were a computer game that was getting the better of him. From the loveseat Bremmer heard the beeps, he heard it ringing as Harvey paced, stretching the long, curly cord. Someone picked up on the other end and Harvey shouted into the receiver.

"You must come quickly! I've apprehended an intruder. He's dangerous. He's agitated. You must come at once!"

The dispatcher asked a question that seemed to puzzle him momentarily. Then he said, "Yes, I know him. His name is Bremmer. He's very agitated. Please come now!"

The voice asked another question and Harvey held the phone against his chest. Addressing Eleanor in the hallway, he asked, "Where does he live?"

Bremmer couldn't see her, but her voice came from a significant remove, as if she were a stranger to both men, forced to watch all this against her will. He also noted that she could only name his street, not his number.

"That's right," Harvey shouted. "I've got him in the house. He's a dangerous man. Please come immediately!"

The worst part, Bremmer thought, was that awful voice, ripe with Scottish pride and injury. The rolled Rs and fatuous privilege. He tried to imagine Harvey speaking Spanish. The voice, he knew, would return to him as the highest horror of the evening.

"Here," he said, standing. "Let me talk to them."

Harvey clapped the phone to its cradle. "Stay where you are! You are not to leave that chair."

Bremmer said, "You're making a mistake. Eleanor doesn't want this. This won't please her."

Harvey clenched his jaw, lifted his bearded chin, and locked his hands on either side of the doorway. "This isn't about you or me or Eleanor," he said. "This is about the right of two people to be happy!"

Bremmer sat down again and thrust his hands into his pockets.

"Still," he said, "you wouldn't have been possible if I hadn't come first."

Harvey pointed at him. "Shut up! You are not to speak or move."

He began to pace a tight circuit before the doorway.

Bremmer glanced over his left shoulder. He couldn't see Eleanor, but he knew she was there. He could feel her willing this scene out of existence. Already she was putting it behind her. Right now, she was suffering. But tomorrow she would not remember. And when the police arrived she'd step out and stand by Harvey's side. It occurred to Bremmer that his friends in the band would be wondering about him. Right about now they'd be setting up on stage, checking their watches, making remarks about what might have detained him. He understood that when the police came he'd be on his own. He supposed he'd always known this moment of denial would come, but somehow he'd needed it. It would be horrible. But it would be the end.

Harvey paced and frowned.

At the sound of an approaching car he paused to listen. The car passed and diminished in the night. Bremmer heard crickets and somewhere down the street someone laughed and a dog barked, almost in unison. Perhaps he'd served judgment on this place, but he'd loved it, too. And now it was saying goodbye to him. Now it belonged to Harvey. For a moment, together, he and Harvey listened to the summer's zenith, the full moon that poured its lunatic music onto the walks and rooftops of the upright town. Outside of themselves, it all made sense.

Bremmer said, "Eleanor? Are you still here, Eleanor?"

Harvey stood and glared. The balefulness of his expression was that Bremmer should single him out for such indignities; that Bremmer should take it upon himself to add this awful coda to the splendid days and nights he'd spent with Eleanor. Couldn't Bremmer see that he didn't deserve this? Couldn't he understand that he, Harvey McGoonan, was just trying to get what the world owed him? With Eleanor he was on the verge, finally, of securing what everybody else had found.

"You are not to speak," Harvey said, and resumed his pacing.

Bremmer watched him. The smells and sounds of the lost season came through the open window. While he listened, there were no human sounds, just the sigh of summer trees in humid darkness, and something else, like the hum of infinitesimal stars forming a dome over this street and its dramas. How bizarre, that the police were travelling through this rare and wonderful night to speak with him. He had the uncertain feeling of having made his point, at last. The point of conclusion and closure that Eleanor had always dodged in fact and denied in her soul, the very crux of their long, debilitating argument. She did not — could not — believe in endings. To acknowledge closure would admit the irrevocable losses of their lives, and therefore that the events themselves held meaning.

But somehow she wasn't here. Once more she'd managed to exempt herself from the present. Was it possible she could sidestep even this? Could she ghost herself out of this one, too?

Another car was coming. He heard it turn onto the street. Harvey paced before the doorway to the kitchen, back and forth.

Bremmer told himself that Eleanor had ceased to matter. Here or not. This would end it. He wished he could step back into that yard full of shrinks and social workers and explain how he'd worked it out. He'd stand on a chair and they'd listen, smiling circumspectly, as he delineated his problem and the novel solution he'd found.

The car slowed in front of the house on the far side, the engine making a hot, panting sound. Harvey continued to pace, oblivious.

Bremmer considered the distance he'd come, the difficult arc he'd negotiated to tie it all up. Earlier in the afternoon he'd stood on a July lawn and tossed a day-glo frisbee back and forth with his therapist. The pink disc had glanced off the grass and risen higher, higher, just beyond Bremmer's fingertips.

From the front door, the rarely-used door at the end of the hall, came two brisk raps.

There was a time, a dense minute of an actual day, when Eleanor had called him "dear," sweet and teasing, and poured wine for him where she had recently refused him water from the tap. How long ago was that? The wine or the water denied — when did it happen?

He felt parched and numb, as if he'd been travelling in circles. The wires had been horribly crossed. Somehow, the water drained the meaning from the wine; somehow the denial reached back and disfigured the former grace.

In the other room Eleanor was talking. Two constables appeared, a man and a woman, much younger than Harvey or Eleanor. They came in without their caps, tall and weighted at the hips with cop equipment, looking slightly lost. Eleanor hesitated behind them. Mid-pace, Harvey looked up, an expectant and preoccupied light on his brow.

The female cop stepped forward, glancing from face to face, and Bremmer rose to shake her hand.

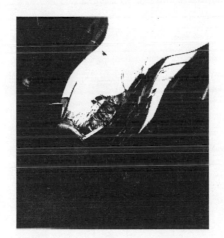

THE END OF ALL OUR SORROWS

There's a moment before I leave the pottery room, just before I close the door and the ovens are cooling and the wheels are still, I hit the switch and the long overhead fluorescents flicker and wink and it feels like lights are going out all over the world. And whatever's been done that day, whatever flawed or unlovely vessel my students have wrought, whatever lie or cliché I've mouthed to encourage otherwise ungifted hands, I leave this place willingly to the darkness.

My actual classes are at night, but this afternoon I monitored the long, slogging studio hours. At five-thirty I walk to my car with that Friday mixture of fatigue and anticipation, though I have no plans for the weekend. The cold engine starts sluggishly and I join the line of cars waiting to exit the lot. The fading autumn sun rims the campus maples with soft orange and yellows; I turn on the radio and try to imagine I'm in high school, walking home with absolutely nothing on my mind: no papers to grade, no lumpy projects to judge. Nothing to worry about, but a heart full of stupid hope and strange belief...

Turning onto the avenue, I notice how the unexpected cold seems to stiffen and silver the vast mowed lawns around the school. The grey cement buildings stand like stones on frozen ground, and I push the pedal to get through the first light. At the next one, where the road meets the entrance to the psychiatric hospital, I'm caught by the red. With one foot on the brake I feed the engine gas to avoid stalling. On the green I gun it into the eastbound lane toward town.

I've been teaching pottery at the community college for three years, and though I'm grateful for the work I've never been one of those educators who accepts proud martyrdom with a paycheque. For one thing, my students are not young, and that sense of forming the raw clay of youth into noble societal commodities was never part of the deal. The men and women who work in my shop are mostly middle-aged, slightly older than myself, and primarily what they're paying for is a sort of therapy, something to do with their hands after their marriages and factory jobs have gone smash. Nothing wrong with that. To me, the late 20th Century is mostly about basket-weaving — false urgencies and paper emergencies to keep adults enticed and preoccupied. To my mind there's little difference between publishing a magazine and making an ashtray. And the latter may last longer. At any rate, down the road there won't be much left besides anger and styrofoam.

Soon after the turn I pass the bus-stop, where woolly mental patients with day passes slump and huddle inside the glass kiosk and baleful teenagers in red berets and jackboots smoke cigarettes nearer the street. A little further on, the old prison leans close to the road with its Victorian towers and spotlights and high walls of cold grey stone. When we were together, Claudette would joke about the proximity of these institutions — prison, psychiatric centre, and community college — and I took her point good-naturedly.

The road levels out and winds leisurely between the lake and stately brick homes. Today the water is like churning chrome, a troubled vibration that will darken quickly in what remains of the light. I turn left and park on a side street. The lake flashes in my mirrors as I get out of the car; as I walk it looms on my shoulder and catches in the corner of my eye, until I gain the upper streets with their enclosed muted tones of brown and ochre brick and reddish autumn trees. A year ago, on an afternoon like this, I'd be heading for Peggy's Grill or The Digestible Pigeon to meet Claudette. Maybe Leo and Pam would turn up later, and after an hour or two of drinks and funny stories Claudette and I would leave together for her house, a supper of pasta and an evening by ourselves.

This afternoon I head toward Bradner's Department Store, the oldest one in town, where I can get a pair of winter boots at a fair price and a jar of instant coffee. The streets are humming and the cold clarifies the smart clip of heels on sidewalks. Somewhere within three city blocks Claudette is finishing her week at the newspaper. She'll be leaving with the managing editor, a florid Australian who wears double-breasted suits, or running last-minute errands alone, maybe buying red wine at the liquor store near the lot where she parks.

A cheerful tourism report issued last year listed our city as the best place to live in the province. Sometimes I can see it. Sometimes in summer when the sidewalks are bustling with visitors who are oblivious to the small and chronic intrigues of this town, I can see its appeal. Even today, a brisk afternoon in late October, the fine old buildings present themselves in dignified relief and the tree-lined streets, civil and clean, lead to residential avenues that seem to promise the ongoingness of things. But not long from now winter will cut the day at noon; numbing winds will roar off the lake and the limestone walls will turn to grey ice, as chilling to see as to touch. Going out will be horrible then, and pity the soul who has no home.

Don't rush it, I tell myself, and I turn toward the store.

Inside, among the first floor aisles of Halloween candy and masks and work clothes, beneath the murky yellow light shed from high ceilings, I compose myself and look around. Raw-faced kids are out of school, milling and shoplifting; old ladies wearing knitted hats like tea cozies are buying sweets and Epsom salts. A guy with the shakes tries on a pair of vinyl gloves from a bin. This must be the last store in the country that still has an elevator with an operator who calls out the goods on each floor. Half a dozen shoppers gather at its ancient doors and wait to ascend. I wait with them, and when the doors rattle open we push into the cramped, fuggy space with lowered faces and involuntary sighs.

I don't recognize the elevator man until we're at the second floor and he calls out the departments in a flat, booming monotone: "Hardware, automotive, kitchen. School supplies and linen." It's Claudette's husband, Steve. Big and grey-bearded, dressed in black with red suspenders and strands of greasy, silver hair trailing beneath his derby hat. I try not to look. But can you believe it? Steve's become the Bradner's elevator man. Steve who met Claudette in this town and travelled the world with her for thirteen years before he broke down and she came back to work in the family china shop. Steve, who left pieces of his mind on windy mountain-tops and in tropical valleys, who tried all the drugs and semi-occult vocations, only to fall back with Claudette to their starting place. Though she eventually pushed him out of the house, the marriage remained legally intact and their lives went along with no admission of fracture. If an old friend stopped Claudette on the street she dutifully reported on Steve's latest enterprise with any wife's interest and enthusiasm. When I asked why they went on this way, she declared, "Nobody divorces around here."

I squeeze into the corner and ride the jerking car to the third and final floor where Steve recites the departments, loud and droning, like a stoned one-man chorus in a Greek tragedy.

He doesn't seem to notice me and I disembark quickly toward men's shoes. The difference between the elvator man and me is that I am angry and he is inert. And because I'm angry Claudette will not see me; because Steve is empty she sees no need for divorce. Mine is no simple case of unrequit-edness or rejection. I'm angry because it was love in the first place. It existed definitely. It signified in our hearts and it should have had substance in the world. She loved me and showed me her love, but she would not show it to the world. She didn't believe in love's ultimate meaning in the world where she worked and ate seafood and parked her car. The reasons for my anger, therefore, also concern the way of the world — they do not begin absolutely in Claudette. But because our love was real and nearly realized she lends them an inevitable form. She has become both the metaphor and the thing itself: the body of a specific hunger and the final figure in a paradigm that denied and squelched my faith. The anger moves between Claudette and the world and fuels itself in a manifold circuit. Claudette flees from its pointless power: she will not see me because she cannot look this aberration in the face. She still meets Steve for dinner once or twice a month. Maybe she even lets him into her bed. But he doesn't worry her because he is gone, because he barely exists.

What Steve and I have in common is that we've both lost the one thing we could not afford to lose.

I lift a pair of waterproof training shoes, light soft leathers with space-age soles, and imagine slipping them on and run-ning forever, over the rooftops of the city and into the trees, down to the bay where Claudette's parents live in a snug bun-galow, then out across the waves in full view of their front window. I hold the shoes and imagine Claudette, a tall, sharp-featured woman of forty, standing with her elderly parents and brothers, watching me stride across the lake of their birth, the water that is the meaning of their lives. My heels raise tiny wings of spray, running until I become a pastel shadow, a ray of winter sunshine, the air itself.

The shoes go back with their fellows and I navigate the aisles toward the cashier and the stairway. At the first landing I look down through the plate glass at the street, at the Friday evening traffic of people together and cars speeding toward occasions of families, lovers, and friends, and I hold my chest against a sudden piercing, as if a great transparent shard had gone through me without a trace. I steady myself on the railing and proceed downward, taking deliberate steps. On the street I squint in the cold air and turn right, up the main drag of stores and restaurants, moving among the purposeful humans, crossing at the light. I turn left, and then down Turnbull, a genteel street where Claudette's family store — now a travel bureau — operated for decades and where I first met her two years ago. The encounter was mostly chance, though I'd been in the shop before and had seen her behind the register or working at an old wooden desk in back. The afternoon we met she was arguing with the Wedgwood salesman, something about prices and stock, and her eyes moved to mine as she spoke. When the salesman left she smiled and shook her head. I happened to know something about the English potteries and asked her about the business. We spoke for almost half an hour and agreed to meet for coffee after work. That's how it started.

A stiffening wind huddles me into the doorway between two display windows set in black tile. On the sidewalk in front of the store a green dragonfly, a refugee from summer, has touched down for the last time. It holds the concrete while the veined wings shiver in the wind like tiny panels of leaded glass. The dragonfly clings to the last current of warmth in the sidewalk that runs parallel to the street and down to the section of cold metal lake visible between the bank and city hall.

I straighten and move away from the store, into the intersection.

A van slides through the yellow light, and as if stepping from behind a secret wall in the middle of the street Steve appears, walking straight at me. Under his arm is an aquarium with a bagged liquor bottle in it. His eyes are hidden beneath the black derby; the raised collars of his peacoat show gaunt cheekbones only. We pass without a nod or word. On the other curb I turn and look after him. Pedestrians give way around the glass tank and the derby swims into the crowd.

Once, discussing Steve's peculiar dereliction, Claudette said, "It would be easier if he had cancer or something. It'd be easier if he was just dead."

Shivering, I start down the next street toward the water and my parked car. Night is closing swiftly and if the traffic isn't bad I'll make it home before the last daylight vanishes.

The place I rent is out beyond the Montreal Road, which runs through an older, impolite part of town that has resisted gentrification: listing redbrick rowhouses with flat tar-paper-roofs, long warehouses full of dead trucks or obsolete plumbing supplies or nothing at all. My turn-off is marked by a stretch of chainlink fence with a few rusty warnings stuck to the mesh, then onto the crumbling company road that pushes straight back half a mile through a shallow jungle of third-growth saplings and weeds. The real estaters call this Light Industrial Acreage, but they will happily parcel it out to any-one desperate enough to make a deal. Another turn onto a dirt lane which emerges abruptly into the white circle of the floodlight that contains the clearing in front of the workshed and the aluminum-sided house.

I park near the trees and let myself into the shed, turning on the lights and space heaters. I sit at the kickwheel, just to steady myself, just to forget the sepulchral voice of Steve in the elevator and the lostness of his figure on the street. The tubs of grog and powder, the rubber trash cans of slip and clay, should speak comfort to me; the little natural-fuel kiln and the shelved biscuit ware and the wheel itself should constitute a higher joy, or at least a pure alternative to suffering. But it's been weeks since I've done anything new or original. My last sustained effort was a series of chamber pots commissioned by an acquaintance who owns a bed-and-breakfast chateau in town. He wanted eight of them to fill with candy and bath beads, one pot for each room. I churned out the order while things were cracking up with Claudette. The ninth pot began when it was clear we were finished. Working, sheer routine, got me through the summer. And in the face of our finality, the inescapable conclusion that our time was over, I kept on with the pot, at first as a matter of distraction. But an idea took hold. A pot of another kind assumed urgent proportions and solidity, the dark side of a love that could find no form, that was scorned and disallowed in this correct and stylish town. Claudette, I realized, was only going with the flow, the way of the world, which is not even fear or greed but self-consciousness to a degree that will hardly let one breathe without irony. The ninth and last pot is a horror of love inverted and a reply to irony, a vengeance of form on possibility denied.

From the wheel, I stare at it sitting in the corner, the deep glaze suffused with bruise-coloured light, its terraced top like a ziggurat set on storm clouds emblazoned with birds, beasts, and our significant numbers. Above and below the glyphs, the bowl is speckled with tiny globules of gold from the ring Claudette gave me, melted down and spattered onto the personal clay like exquisite shrapnel, like the essence of our love exploded. All of this was summer's last expression, founded in a bafflement and grief so large as to be almost historical. The pot contains the coming together and violent rift of hearts and seasons. It holds the topmost convolutions of our desire and plans, the thin rim where these meet our darker, essential selves, and the depth of fear and fixed will that makes them all for naught. If you lift the fantastic lid you might find this bowl filled with eternal fire, the secret combustibles of faith and futility that cannot be quenched. The glory and the nadir that is everything.

If I love this pot it is because this pot contains my love. If I am addicted to my anger — if I actually need it — the reason lies in the absence and availability of forms. Love has few, and fewer still are respectable. Anger is one of the last imperatives to be officially recognized. In this smart leaden town, anger is a currency they cannot deny.

Rising from the wheel, I step over to the pot and take it in my hands. I leave the studio with it, move through the outer cold and artificial light, and set the pot at my feet while I let myself into the house. Inside, I place the pot on the table in the centre of the main room. The room remains dark while I start dinner in the kitchen.

At eight o'clock the telephone rings. It's Leo.

"Cliff," he says, "are you there? Are you out there, Cliff?"

"I'm here."

"Just wanted to make sure you hadn't glazed yourself or drowned in a barrel of slip."

Leo lives in town and sculpts in neon. His wife is top administrator in the public library system; her schedule and income allow Leo to sleep days and labour through the night with tubing, gas, and electricity in his attic workshop. He is the only man in the world I envy, unless Claudette is already with someone new.

"Listen," he says, "why not drive over here and we'll hit a few bars. Next thing you know it'll be winter and you won't want to leave the house."

I'm sitting at the kitchen table with the phone in one hand, a sandwich in the other, looking at the darkly gleaming pot in the next room. The light through the doorway glosses the burnished contours. It could be anything, standing there on the other table: a crematorial urn, a sacred font, one of those hellish walking eggs from Hieronymus Bosch.

"I don't think I'm going anywhere this evening," I tell Leo. "I believe I'll sit tight."

"Come on, man. I'm worried about you. Come over and check out the cross. It's nearly finished. That green stuff really sizzles and spits. We'll take it out on the roof and plug it in."

I try to envision myself on Leo's roof with a neon cross.

"Thanks, but I don't think so. Not tonight."

Leo sighs. He says, "I keep telling you, there's no point in suffering. It's not necessary. All you have to do is manage that little Zen twist. One neat emotional zigzag that will get you off the hook. It's all in your head. No one wants your pain, Cliff. Your pain is of no earthly use."

"Maybe not. But it exists, and I'm stuck with it."

The ninth pot, shining softly beyond the doorway, perhaps the last pot I'll ever make, was shaped from raw clay that Claudette and I excavated from creekbanks that feed into the lake, sites of her youth she shows few and still visits for spiritual refuge in summer. While Leo talks I think about the way we mined the grey, sinuous stuff into aluminum tubs; when we swam in deeper pools we found the same clay on the bottom. We'd dive and bring up dripping fistfuls which we smeared on our faces, necks and collar-bones as if it had medicinal qualities, as though it could suck out the bad buzz of civilization and return us to our sane and loving selves.

"You haven't seen her, have you?" I ask. "Have you seen her around lately?"

"Claudette? No, not me. But Pam talked to her the other day. They were supposed to get together tonight, but Claudette's women's group was meeting at her house."

We listen to each other's silence over the wire. I know Leo is wishing he hadn't said that. He's wondering if he gave anything away. He continues, speaking fast.

"Anyhow, it won't do any good to stew. But if you don't want to come over, that's fine. Looks like a rotten night, as a matter of fact. I think I see rain out there."

"Thanks for calling," I say. "I'm not up for much right now."

"All right. Sure. Call me sometime. Why suffer?"

He gives me a chance to answer, and when I don't we say goodnight and I hang up the phone.

He's right about the weather. A fine, hard rain whips

against the window and the wind lightly rattles the pane. I put on my coat and stand before the pot in the other room. I can hear Claudette say, "What are you doing, Cliff? What's going on?" I gather the pot under my arm and step outside to the porch. The wind tosses the tall weeds and the rain slants against my face. I walk over the wet, spotlit gravel to the car and set the pot on the passenger side. In a series of ragged manoeuvres, I turn the car around and drive into the rain and darkness. My heart beats twice as fast as the wipers and I feed the engine to keep it from stalling. If it dies now it won't start without a push, and there's no time for that. Now, there is no time.

Driving toward town, it's hard not to look at the pot riding beside me in the dark. Why didn't I foresee the danger in shaping it from the clay of Claudette's history, the original opaque material of her silent girlhood and taciturn adolescence? Despite the seminars and career changes, the new hair and wardrobe, she is still this substance, though its meaning changed the moment she shared it with me. Why did she deny that moment? How could she be so naive as to think she could show me this world and let me love it, then take it back as though that moment had never occurred? For this pot is nothing less than the living world, and though its stars and griffins and the tall, levelled lid are inventions of my own terrible urgency, the initial impulse began as belief in our ability to make it new and useful. Whether the fault lies in the pride of her clay or the heat of my terror, together we have made something profane from that thwarted belief. Selfishly and unconsciously, we have created an ark of broken covenants, a shell of fire wherein nullity is stored. This is the error of our time and the malaise of this place. This is the world, which begs to be destroyed.

With a hand washed pale in passing headlights, I lift the awkward lid and dare myself to look. Driving one-handed and peering through the wipers and rain, I ask, "What was that other goal? What was the better thing we were waiting for?"

Without looking inside, I lower the lid on the vibrating pot and drive.

Claudette lives on the heights outside of town in an old stone house. None of the half-dozen houses near hers was built in the last three decades and most are made from the same grey sediment. These are inhabited by hip young professors or city politicians or proud old women who'll turn their dogs on a stranger. When the weather turns cold these cheerless stones take on the aspect of tombs and ruins. At Christmas the bitter wind off the lake below rattles the coloured lights on stunted trees and the setting feels like a Mexican graveyard on an English moor. From the open window of my car the black lake and the city in the rainy distance behind it are like something unreal but familiar I might dream five or ten years from now.

I'm parked at the crossroads above her house, staring at the light in her windows. I shouldn't be here. I should put it in gear and go home.

Instead, I kill the engine and feel the cold rain that blows into the car. I listen to the wind in the big, craggy trees that bend around the street lamp and cast perturbed shadows on the road that descends to Claudette's house. This is a night when none of us should be out. A time when any act will become bigger than its intent, and mere words will vanish over the dark water.

But I notice the cars parked behind me and across the way — Volvos and Toyotas and four-wheel-drive wagons — and a high warble of laughter floats up the street. There's movement behind the half-drawn shades.

The car door shuts with a dull thud. For a minute I stand beside the vehicle, waiting and listening, with the chamber pot in my arms. Then I proceed into the shifting shadows and the wind and down the road into the darker, solid shadow of the house. The nearest window is open two inches; women's voices, clear and tart, drift out with cigarette smoke. I flatten my back to the wet stone and slide down into a crouch, the pot cradled in my lap. Inside, they're talking about their jobs and their cottages and the New Paganism. They are complaining about the mayor and the endless rain. The cold stone supports me while they talk and laugh about a hundred small items that will never touch my life. They are lawyers and therapists and newspaper women, and their talk is like sweet muzak, a string ensemble that plays only melody, and only the melodies that reach us while we're otherwise engaged. Behind their talk is an unconscious faith in the things hands have made and a heavy investment in the abstract routines of business. Their talk is loaded with banality and breezy swagger and the partially disguised unctions of sex — a vestigial intimacy they have learned to deflect because the soil is never as welcoming as it seems. I hear every word, all the tones of their hope and disenchantment. And then Claudette says:

"I meant to tear them out and put in new ones, but Cliff kept showing up. Whenever I found the energy to work outside, presto, he'd materialize, standing there goofy and forlorn. There was so little good weather anyhow. I lost the whole summer that way."

These are her words. Better than the women in her living room, I know what she means.

With the pot against my chest, I slip around to the side, up the porch steps with an even, soundless tread. The door is unlocked, as I knew it would be, and when I'm inside the kitchen I think, How nice, how pleasant, with wine bottles and flowers; how good it might be to call this place home. Was I ever welcome here? Was there ever a time when she filled my glass or led me upstairs?

I move toward the talk, the racy laughter. Suddenly, in the doorway to the other room, a woman's face comes close to mine. Her hands cover the front of her silk shirt and she says, "Christ, you startled me." And then, backing away with her eyes on the dripping blue pot: "Claudette, there's someone here."

She retreats into the living-room that's hazed with smoke, littered with wine glasses and women's shoes. The busy voices falter and fade. Claudette looks up from the circle of her sisters, her face rigid and lined but still tan. She moves her hand through her short black hair and leans forward as if to rise, but she doesn't. She knows that she is safer, less herself, if she remains with the group in chairs.

"Oh hell," she says. "What is it, Cliff? Why are you here?"

The others watch and wait for my answer. They are handsome women in their late thirties and early forties, professional women with votes and expensive cars. Their faces are neither hostile nor open. A few register something like grim anticipation and dour humour; the rest are blank, a little tired and put out at the prospect of a surprise.

I stand before them, at the edge of their circle, and raise the pot toward the ceiling. I want to tell them about the world they have forgotten, the world within the world they traffic in, the world full of dark and unholy fire. And that other world without, the true third world of indifferent rain that falls on the void. I want them to see that the form of these worlds fashioned on the humble wheel is the only answer to those who have never worked in rain and fire, faith and disappointment. It is the only answer to those who choose not to notice the existence of a love that might join these disparate elements to make meaning again. This is the vessel of our rage and the shape of our grief, the love you would not countenance become an awful beauty.

Claudette says, "You shouldn't be here, Cliff. This is not for you."

Their eyes stay on the upraised pot as if to stay it against the inevitable with intelligence and rectitude. I step forward and enter the circle: their smooth oval faces shift slightly in a unified gaze that seems to regard the changing space between us, the perfumed smoke that invites and proscribes, the bright terror of possibility that was always there. This raised vessel is not only the essence of my loss but also the figure of all our love, the human potential which anger and inertia cannot indefinitely deny. If I smashed it now the crash would be huge. Blue shards of sky would flay their slender ankles and scatter their empty shoes. But that possibility, that love they crave and deride —would it be shattered? Would it leave us forever?

"Don't Cliff," Claudette says. "Please. This is my house."

I look at her and at each wondering face. Whatever they say later, we know at this moment that we are in the grip of something here. We'll assign winners and losers later, but in this moment we are together.

I lower the pot and hold it forward as if to implore them with its signs and numerals, its terraced lid like the familiar city their business is in. Standing there, braced and repelled on the bright centre of their single will, I almost remember something. An echo of summer. Laughter on the telephone. The way Claudette's face softened immediately after sex to reveal a girlish overbite she never showed in the secular day.

"You didn't know us, but we were lovers here," I tell them. "None of you knew it, but she loved me then. She really did."

Their arms, heavy with bracelets against hands holding cigarettes and drinks, dangle over the chair rests. Hands capable of mockery and sweet attentions.

"You should have blessed us while it was still love," I tell them. "None of it would matter if it hadn't been real. But for the good of us all, you should have blessed it while there was still love and time."

There is no reading their eyes now. They watch me with a keenness no one watching them might understand. It might be fear, or exhilaration, or triumph. Right now, there's no telling. Right now, between us, there are no signs.

Claudette says, "For God's sake, Cliff. For God's sake."

I stand there and hold the pot toward them.

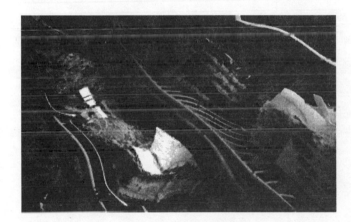

THE WAR IN HEAVEN

About two hours before the party was supposed to start Carl got a call from Rosemary. He heard the phone ringing through the roar of his mother's ancient vacuum cleaner and for a moment he stood there, trying to decide if the sound was real. Twice already he'd switched off the machine, thinking he heard the phone, only to find silence. This time he turned it off and rushed to the telephone in the kitchen. His hello was breathless and tinged with something like suspicion.

"Hello Carl," she said, her rich English voice heavy on the first syllable and charmingly soft on the last. "It's me," she said. "I only have a minute to tell you that I'm bringing a friend to the party. She's the most fascinating woman, a photographer who's been living in Paris, and she's anxious to meet everyone. I know you'll love her."

Carl could hear the restaurant noises in the background,

the clatter of plates against raised voices.

"She came in at the end of my shift and we got talking. She told me she'd love to photograph me. I'll tell you all about it later. You'll adore her. Now I must rush…"

"Hold on," Carl said.

"I'll see you tonight —"

And she was gone.

Carl went back to his cleaning. As he walked the vacuum back and forth over the living room, his sense of annoyance grew. Typical Rose, throwing him a curve at the last moment. She should have asked him before inviting a stranger. This was his mother's house and the point of the party was a joke — a suburb party to show his friends where he'd been living for the past six weeks, to have an ironic laugh at strange old Carl in a neat little bungalow with plaid furniture and bad paintings and pastel carpets. He'd even selected a stack of his mother's records from the early Sixties — Herb Alpert, Floyd Cramer, Acker Bilk — instrumentals that were so corny they were almost hip. None of this, he worried, might be precisely appropriate for entertaining a stranger. He wanted the evening to go smoothly: it marked a sort of reintroduction of Rosemary to the circle, the first time they'd all been together since she'd gone into the clinic.

He turned off the machine again and stepped back into the kitchen while the old vacuum shut down with a fading whine and rattle, as if there was a BB ricocheting through the tinny complexities of its engine. He breathed deeply and stared at the phone. No point in calling Rosemary back: she'd be gone by now, on her way home or to some other rendezvous he didn't want to know about. Besides, his new approach was to avoid confrontation, to ignore lesser snags and gaffes for the greater good of their connection and her happiness. Those two weeks in the clinic back in the summer, they meant something. She didn't go there because she was irresponsible or stupid. The crisis had been real: she'd lost her job and her children had gone to live with strangers, and it was imperative now that he prove his reliability. She needed him, and though he knew she wouldn't admit it, she had given him a second chance to participate in her complicated life. He mustn't let her down by succumbing to his chronic doubts and paranoias: these had contributed to their initial breakup back in the spring, before she'd lost it, and he didn't want to make the same mistake twice.

He put the vacuum cleaner away and headed for the shower. Before he turned on the water he went down the short flight of stairs and took the phone off the hook. Standing there naked he regarded the instrument as the source of many troubles, the vehicle of particular woe. Rosemary could call him, but he could never reach her at home. It would ring and ring and he'd envision her glancing distractedly at the call display, grimacing and returning to her reverie, disappointed it wasn't bigger game.

"Stop it, Carl," he said, as though he were speaking to himself on the phone. "Stop thinking that way." And he went back upstairs and stepped under the hot, stinging water.

Mitch and Carrie, who had moved to an isolated house in the country about the same time Carl had given up his apartment to live in the suburbs, were the first to arrive. They'd never seen his mother's house and they smiled circumspectly as he showed them the small upholstered rooms with their souvenir pillows and lamps and the bric-a-brac his mother had brought back from Florida. Mitch was a social worker, a strenuously placid character with a broad patriarchal beard and a squarely contained horror of dysfunction. He looked into the rooms as if each held exactly what he expected, and these contents neither pleased nor dismayed him. Carrie, who published a small magazine on rural living from their house, laughed politely at the family photographs of departed pets and the studio portrait of Carl from high school. The latter prompted Mitch to make a few technical comments: his extra-professional passion was the photography which in recent years had become a cleanly antidote to the disorder of his day job. He took pictures with an oversized German view camera, an imposing two-handed contraption with an extending snout and tripod. To see him operating in the field, often hidden under a black hood as he gauged the variables of time and light, put Carl in mind of Civil War photographers. Primarily Mitch avoided human subjects, preferring portraits of trees and clouds and ice formations, immensely detailed images that caught the clean abstract patterns in nature.

"That reminds me," Carl said as they filed down the stairs to the kitchen. "Rosemary is bringing a new friend tonight. Another photographer."

"Rosemary?" Mitch said. "You invited Rosemary?"

"I told you she was coming," Carrie said. "You knew that."

Mitch shrugged.

Carrie said, "Carl knows what he's doing."

"Do I?" Carl said. "Well, she's been pretty isolated since she's been sick. I know she's really missed everyone. I know she's looking forward to seeing you guys again."

Neither Carrie nor Mitch said anything. Carl led them to the refrigerator and handed them cans of beer.

"Anyhow," he said. "The photographer is Rosemary's discovery. I've never met the woman."

The doorbell rang. Stan Tryfonopoulos, a curly-headed young composer who also played a romantic oboe in the local symphony, came in with his wife, Amy. On the way they'd picked up Allen Dent, who owned the bookstore where Carl worked. Allen immediately assumed the La-Z-Boy in the corner: he set an ornate glass dish from the coffee table on his knee and began to roll a cigarette. Carl brought out more beer and promised pizza for later. He put an old Sergio Mendez record on his mother's Mediterranean-style cabinet stereo while most of the group settled in chairs around the living room. Stan paced between them, his face lit with genuine delight.

"This is great," he said, looking around. "I love it. I love these paintings. Like those framed landscapes in motels."

The doorbell rang again. Amy parted the curtain on the picture window and looked out as a cab reversed down the driveway.

"I think it's Rosemary," she said.

Carl opened the door at the side of the house. Rosemary entered in a long woolen coat with the collar up, smiling and smelling of sweet perfume. Another woman was behind her. In the entranceway Rosemary gave Carl a glancing peck on the cheek and stepped aside.

"Carl," she said, "I want you to meet my friend, Leah Silver. Leah, this is the famous Carl."

His first thought was that the name sounded like an alias. Leah Silver. What kind of name was that? Then he realized he'd seen her before, in the drugstore or post office. He had noted something in her bearing, her movement, that reminded him of Rosemary. In the electric glare of the entranceway he could see that she was ten years Rosemary's senior, maybe fifty-two or three. Her face was utterly impassive, almost waxen. But the body was Rosemary's, a perfect match.

Carl moved to take Rosemary's heavy coat; she stepped out of it theatrically while it was in his hands and took three long strides into the main room as if to announce herself. She wore a black silk blouse and purple harem pants and immediately, with Mitch and Carrie staring, she flicked off her shoes in two deft movements. She embraced Stan as if she'd just returned from a cruise she must tell him about.

Then she turned around and said, "Everybody, I'd like you to meet my new friend, Leah Silver. She's been taking wonderful pictures in China. And before that she lived in Paris."

Leah had just given her coat to Carl; she drifted into the room with Rosemary standing proudly behind her.

"Paris," Stan said. "What a town. Amy and I went there on our honeymoon."

The pale woman in the long black dress stood before them and nodded slowly. She said something in a small, precise voice that seemed to come from some other part of the room. The younger people leaned toward her.

Rosemary interjected: "Leah has the most divine studio down at the old mill, near my place. She has the whole tower, and it's full of lovely books and music and photographs." Rosemary laughed as she sat down on the sofa. "Well, I haven't actually seen it yet. But from what Leah tells me it sounds like heaven."

Leah nodded with a sideways cant, as though she were listening carefully to her own words: "Yes," she said, "it's a haven for me. It's my work place, my darkroom, but it's a real retreat."

Her voice was over-mild and pliant, wholly without edges. It seemed to Carl like the voice of a plant rather than a person. Against the bossa nova on the stereo it reminded him of a creeper twining around an ornate trellis. He moved a chair toward her and asked what she'd like to drink.

"Just some water," she said as she lowered herself into the chair.

"Is tap water all right?"

She stared and blinked at him. "Maybe coffee," she said.

In a very different voice, Stan said, "Hey, we brought Twister in honour of the evening's theme. Who wants to play?"

The game was set up while Carl made coffee and stacked more records. Everyone but Allen and Leah took off their shoes and got down on the carpet. Mitch assumed a cross-legged posture beside the plastic mat where he called out the numbers and colours that dictated where the players put their hands and feet. He looked God-like and bemused as they balanced and contorted, toppled and fell, one by one. Allen, who claimed sleep-deprivation, smoked and worked a crossword puzzle; Leah perched fragilely on the corner of the sofa, sipping her coffee while she observed the game. She had particularly asked Carl for a cup and saucer, and he'd had to dig into one of his mother's cabinets to oblige her.

At the end of several rounds Rosemary and Stan were the only ones left on the mat. Stan blushed as he arched himself over Rosemary's hips, according to commands from Mitch. She lifted herself half-an-inch to make contact. Her grey and copper hair fell over her face and she held the position without straining. The moment prolonged itself while Carl and the others watched. Carl took small breaths and waited. Mitch glanced in his direction and he knew Mitch and the rest had been right when they'd asked him, "What are you doing with Rosemary? What are you thinking?" If he had to answer that one he'd say that he was thinking about the day she reappeared after weeks of silence and the subsequent breakdown. It was also the day he'd received a cheque for a couple thousand from the estate of a deceased uncle, a renewal of funds that brought a surge of fresh hope and prompted Allen to give him the afternoon off. Carl cashed several hundred and walked over to an outdoor restaurant to celebrate. There he ran into a pair of women he knew and bought them a bottle of wine and a plate of spring rolls. The afternoon waned into laughter and pleasant flirtations when suddenly, like a slightly altered but familiar dream, Rosemary materialized behind his shoulder in a sleeveless little dress, her hair loose, her bare arms tanned and slender. He heard the bright schoolgirlish laugh before he saw her. Sitting there, he turned toward the voice and caught her perfume in the open air. He recognized her in a haze of late afternoon sunlight that fell on the courtyard — Rosemary standing against the light with moonstones on her fingers and another on a silver strand against her collarbone, her dishevelled and greying hair splayed on her thin, square shoulders. Her face and arms were thinner than he remembered, too. Before he could speak she laughed and cupped her hand over his, and without a second thought he rose and left with her. He walked beside her, listened to her whimsical little questions and declarations, slightly stunned by the sensation of Rosemary coming back to him all at once. In another dream-like transition they were seated on the patio of a different restaurant down by the river, a place they'd happily frequented when their affair was in full swing, and he ordered martinis and oysters as in former days and she supplied the opalescent laughter and those quirky Rosemary remarks that barely made sense, misusing words such as "pratfall" and "snafu," turning verbs into nouns and vice versa, protesting cheerily when he pronounced her error. At the end of the meal she dragged him off to a club where she danced with half a dozen stunt pilots who were in town for an air show. And even then, watching them, he'd slammed his hand to his forehead and muttered, "Idiot! Fool!" But after she'd danced with all six, after she'd absorbed their astonished grins and hungry stares, she slipped her arm into his and informed him that he was taking her home. And he did. God help him, he drove to her new place in the jungly public housing down by the water as if those two months were blips, inconsequential static on the screen. The only clue came just before she got out, when she leaned back and stared through the windshield at the slow discoloured river and said, "That time in the hospital was unavoidable. I was very, very tired. But I can't go back. Ever. If I do I'll lose everything. This is my last chance." Then she kissed him lightly on the cheek and ran across the lot to her bedraggled townhouse.

Mitch read the next move and Rosemary extended a leg between Stan's; Stan stretched his left arm to the limit and twisted his head and shoulders backward. His eye met Carl's. He opened his mouth, frowned, and let himself collapse.

"Hey, you!" Rosemary shouted at him. "You gave up!"

She fell back on her elbows, panting a little. "The men always give up on me!" she cried.

Stan rose self-consciously and shook his head.

"The men always quit," Rosemary said, still sprawled on the brightly coloured mat.

Leah sipped her coffee and watched. They heard the particular clink her cup made when she set it on the saucer she held above her lap.

The last act of the party featured Rosemary doing a slow, interpretive dance to "Stranger On The Shore" in the middle of the living room. Carl watched her slim bare feet ply the bluish pastel carpet, her red-painted toes clenching the stiff pile, and he remembered her bodily genius for turning the laughable into the sublime, for transforming dumb muzak into sweet experience, somehow skewing the whole enterprise of irony. The display struck him as unbearably poignant and he felt grateful relief when the record ended and she tumbled laughingly to the sofa.

Just before midnight they stood in the entranceway, donning coats and thanking Carl. Stan slapped him on the back Mitch took his leave with a firm, wordless handshake, his eyes narrowed and knowing above his beard. Rosemary said, "Thank you, dahling..." in her best movie star voice as he reinvested her with her heavy woolen coat. She left the house in front of Leah, who proffered her strangely cool and plant-like hand. Leah peered at him and said, "You know where my studio is? The mill tower, near Rosemary's? You must visit me." Carl felt that she was willing him to look into her eyes. He had not noticed before, but up close he saw that they were arid and outlined in cakey black mascara, like the eyes of an ancient Mandarin or gypsy. Still, her body was supple and winsome.

"Come tomorrow," she said, almost whispering, "or the day after. I often stay late."

She withdrew her hand and he thanked her for the invitation.

After everyone had said goodnight, after he had closed and locked the door, Carl stood there and listened to their muffled voices from the driveway. Then the sound of car doors and motors starting. He put some things in the refrigerator and rinsed Leah's coffee cup and the cut-glass dish Allen had used for ashes. The rest he'd leave until morning.

Later, almost the moment he'd turned off the lamp beside his bed, the telephone rang. He rose quickly and felt his way down through the dark to the kitchen.

"So," Rosemary said, "was it a success? Did you have a good time?"

"I guess so," he said. "I think it went all right."

He reached for a chair and sat down. Almost all of his real conversations with Rosemary took place on the phone now.

"Everyone was very nice to me," she said. "Well, Mitch was a little distant. And didn't you think it odd that he never talked to Leah about cameras or photography or anything? But I love cranky old Allen, and Stan is always a doll."

"They were all happy to see you again. It's been a while."

"Yes," she said. "It's been a long time since I've seen my friends." He could sense her mind drifting out in the dark, turning over scenes of the evening. She laughed and came back to herself.

"Was I beautiful?" she asked.

"Were you beautiful? Yes. Of course. You knocked them dead. You were totally lovely."

She sighed a genuine, audible sigh.

"That's good," she said. "I'm glad."

He held the phone and listened to her silent contentment. He imagined her bedroom with the antique lamp and the light diffused through a peach-coloured shade fitted with a garland of linked angels.

"But you know," she said, "I think they were just a tad leery of me. Just a tad. I think they don't know what to make of us — of you and me, I mean. They don't know what's going on between us."

Carl laughed. "Why should they? We don't know what it is ourselves."

He could hear her shift the receiver to her other hand. He knew she was getting comfortable in her bed.

"But didn't you love Leah?" she asked. "I think the gods sent her to me. I just know we're going to be the dearest friends. A week ago I spotted her walking down the cinder road to her studio, and I thought, 'Who's that? She doesn't come from around here.' I've been waiting for a woman friend like her for ages."

"Sure," Carl said. "She seemed nice enough."

"Oh, Carl! She was more than nice. Didn't you think she

was beautiful? And she wants to photograph me. She says I could get modelling jobs. She used to be a model herself in the Sixties, she was on the cover of something, and she says she knows I could get work."

Carl sat in the dark kitchen. The summer had been long and draining. He'd worked and waited for Rosemary to come back. Somehow, in the face of common sense, he had kept faith. Sitting there, listening to her, he wondered about that faith. He wondered if that was the right word for the thing that kept him going.

"Anyhow," she continued, "it was wonderful to see those sweet people again. I've missed them so much," she said with real emotion. "I hope they know how much I've missed them."

"They know," Carl said.

He asked her to meet him at the bookstore after work tomorrow. She agreed, though Carl wasn't confident she'd remember the date. He realized she was falling asleep on the other end. She began talking to her stuffed bear in slurred babytalk: Carl's foreboding vanished, replaced by a fresh wave of acute poignancy.

"I'll always have Mumbles," she said to her bear, "won't I, Mumbles! Mumbles will never break my heart..."

"Goodnight, Rose," Carl said, pronouncing her name softly into the mouthpiece. "Better sleep, now. You need your sleep."

"Goodnight," she said thickly, fading fast. "Night, Carl..."

He listened to her fumble the receiver, the connection breaking with an awkward plop, as though she'd dropped the phone into deep, forgetful water.

Around five the next afternoon, Carl was sticking prices into piles of new books at the desk near the front window. The late autumn sunshine was like golden smoke on the store-fronts and the sidewalks and several times he thought he heard Rosemary's laughter outside. Business was slow and Carl found it difficult to keep his mind on the chore. He wanted to be outside. He wanted to be in some other place, some other city or country, with Rosemary, listening to her talk about food or weather or architecture, sharing her physical excitement about the world.

A customer left and the store was suddenly empty. Allen appeared from the back and leaned on the desk. He rolled and lit a cigarette and looked out the window.

"If you could sell days like this we'd be millionaires," he said. He reached for an ashtray behind the cash machine. "You don't have to finish that this afternoon," he said. "It can wait."

"I'm supposed to meet Rosemary here. There's a fifty-fifty chance she'll actually turn up."

Allen lifted an eyebrow and squinted at him through the cigarette smoke. He said, "After we dropped her off last night there was some speculation in the car as to the exact nature of your connection with her now."

Carl slapped a book shut and laughed. "It's strange," he said. "In her mind, we're not a couple. She's free to wander. But we actually spend more time together now than we did a year ago. It's very strange."

"I can see how she'd get bored," Allen said as he glanced again at the street.

Carl looked at him.

"I mean," Allen said, "she's obviously accustomed to a faster pace. The way she dresses, the things that interest her. I know she doesn't have money, but obviously it comes to her in cycles. Obviously she craves the stimulation."

"Stimulation?" Carl shook his head. "Christ, they had to sedate her in the hospital. And now she's talking about becoming a model. This new woman, Leah, told her she could make it in modelling. I just don't know."

"I guess I appreciate your concern," Allen said. He scratched his beard and stared out the window. A kid on a bicycle sailed through the intersection with his arms folded carelessly to his chest.

"I know how I must sound," Carl said. "But I know things about her nobody else does. And I'm telling you, this talk about taking her picture is not healthy. Not now. People have taken pictures of her before, and it didn't turn out well."

"She's had trouble," Allen said abstractedly.

"You don't know the half. Hell, I don't know half of it."

Allen frowned and blanked his cigarette in the ashtray. He straightened and pushed a fist into his lower back and drifted toward the far end of the store.

The light was going grey when Carl spotted Rosemary coming down the street. She was wearing a tweed jacket and jeans, and to watch her walk, to see her moving through the people with her head high, her stride brisk and purposeful and her arms held gracefully at her side, you would never guess the violation and pain she had endured — or invited — or the waves of both she had navigated in her beautiful, witless way. He shoved the stacks of books under the desk and grabbed his coat. They met just outside the door.

"Carl!" she cried, laughing. "Oh, I'm sorry. I know I'm late. I just had to pick up a few things."

"That's all right," he said.

"I must show you. I bought the most wonderful things."

The burnish of her jacket and the sound of her laughter in the cooling air almost persuaded him that they were meant for each other, that indeed they were a couple as other men and women made couples. There on the sidewalk she showed him several items she'd bought in nearby shops: beeswax candles and a bar of lavender soap and new gloves for the coming winter. She held the tissue-wrapped soap out for him to sniff.

"Isn't that lovely?" she said.

She brought the soap to her nose and inhaled luxuriantly. Passers-by looked back and smiled.

She returned the soap to her sack and said, "I told Leah to meet us here. You don't mind, do you? I thought we could all get a drink. She'll be here any minute."

Carl took a deep breath and listened to her talk in bright tones about the comings and goings of her day, the small inconveniences and shifts of luck.

He looked down the street.

"Here she comes," he said.

Rosemary stopped and turned. "What did you say?"

"Here comes Leah."

The other woman came toward them in cool, jaunty steps, with a leather bag over her shoulder. From the distance she moved and looked like a much younger woman, something like an undergraduate insouciance in her gait.

Carl watched them embrace. Leah reached into her bag and brought out a silk scarf she'd purchased that afternoon.

"Oh, it's exquisite!" Rosemary said, pulling the scarf between her fingers.

For minutes on the street corner there was a discussion of textures and colours and best buys, with Leah's soft, meticulous voice flowing around Rosemary's delighted exclamations.

Leah laid her plant-like hand on Rosemary's wrist.

"Listen," she said, "I'm on my way back to the tower. Would you like to see it? I can make espresso. Would you be interested, Carl?"

"He can drive us," Rosemary said. "Where's your car, Carl? Is it far from here?"

Carl looked up and down the street. Clouds like black smoke had collected to the west. Already it was nearly dark.

"Sure," he said. "I'm parked on the other block. We can walk there."

"Oh, I've been looking forward to this," Rosemary said. "Ever since you described the place."

Leah nodded slowly and said, "Good. Good. We'll have coffee in the tower and I'll show you some things."

The women lagged a step behind Carl, shoulder to shoulder, speaking fast and low, their heads slightly inclined. Driving through the rush-hour traffic Carl fiddled with the radio. Rosemary had insisted that Leah ride in front with him. He turned the radio off and steered deliberately through the congested streets. In fifteen minutes they were in the north end: Rosemary told Carl to turn onto the unpaved road, an old rail bed of cinders that made a short cut to where she lived. The studio, she said, was just down the cinder road from her house.

"I know," said Carl. "I know where it is."

The night had grown dark, a nearly full moon sliding in and out of dramatic black clouds over the river to their right.

"Slow down," Rosemary said. "We want to see that moon." She leaned forward from the back seat. Carl could smell her perfume. "What a sky," she said. "This town doesn't deserve such a sky."

Leah made a feathery cooing sound.

"Slow down, Carl," Rosemary said.

He touched the brake and felt the moon's intrusive stare over the glazed water and the infrequent trees, skinny and black along the river bank.

"Oh, wow," Rosemary said.

Carl slowed the car and gazed with the women at the anxious light on the drab, abandoned landscape. The river turned slightly away and a field of scrub brush and broken glass swept unevenly toward the old mill, monolithic and imposing like a castle in silhouette. To the left, just above the cinder road, the low-rent townhouses where Rosemary lived stood isolated in the dark, an orange bulb burning dimly over each porch.

"The mill looks nice in moonlight, don't you think?" Leah asked in her small, precise voice.

There was a banging thud as if someone had punched the car and he felt the faintest tremor go through the wheel in his hands.

"Jesus, what was that?"

The women seemed to ponder the question briefly. The second rock hit the hood just inches from the windshield and he saw it ricochet into the night.

"What the hell," Carl said, and he poured on the gas. The car fishtailed in the cinders.

"What the hell's going on?"

"Those kids," Rosemary said, looking back. "Kids from my complex hide in the bushes down there. The cops came around last night."

"Why didn't you —" He looked in the rearview and shook his head. "I should go back," he said. "I'll park the car and go after them. The little bastards. They could have killed us."

There was a silence as the car sped bumpily down the road toward the mill. Then Rosemary said, "But don't you want to see the studio, Carl?"

"What?"

"Can't you just leave it for now?"

"You'll enjoy yourself in the tower," Leah said. "I'll make coffee. It might be better just to let it go, Carl."

The primness in her voice made Carl self-conscious about his anger. He didn't want to seem hyper about his car.

"They could have killed us," he said, less emphatically.

"Come on, Carl," Rosemary said, and Leah directed him into the parking lot. The half-dozen cars there were Saabs and BMWs and one shiny little sports car that gleamed under the spotlights like a golden egg. When he got out he saw the crater in his car's hood. He swore and touched the fist-sized dent.

"I really ought to go after those kids," he said.

"Come on," Rosemary coaxed, tugging on his sleeve. The expensive cars and the Gothic quality of the building itself seemed to excite her. Carl looked back at his automobile. A cold fog was rising over the river and infiltrating the industrial wasteland that surrounded the premises.

"You'll love it up here," Leah told him.

She inserted the card key into the heavy door. It opened electronically and they entered a wide tiled lounge that fronted a corridor studded with brass pots and green, damp-looking ferns. Carl paused to glance at the directory on the wall. The mill had been wholly gentrified, done over to accommodate computer companies, dating agencies, even a rock-climbing studio on the west wing of the ground floor.

"I love it already," Rosemary said. "I feel like this is where I belong."

"This way," Leah said, and she led them down the corridor to the elevator. They stepped in and Leah pressed the top button for the third floor. The elevator itself was clean and brass-fitted, designed to look like it was a hundred years old. Somehow its gilded edges reminded Carl of old cash registers he'd seen in barbershops when he was a kid.

"Imagine coming to work here every day," Rosemary said in a dreamy, yearning voice. "Why, it wouldn't be like work at all!"

Leah smiled coolly. "Then you must visit me whenever you're able."

The doors opened and they stepped out onto a floor of sanded but unfinished wood. Across the hall a diffused electric light shone through the scalloped glass door scripted with *Imagio Productions*.

"Down here," Leah said. She turned a corner and worked a regular key into the door to her studio. She reached for a switch and a long fluorescent flickered and lit the space. In her small, formal voice she said, "Please. Come in."

Rosemary entered looking up and down, smiling with wonder and pleasure like a child.

"Nice," said Carl, just behind her. "Very nice."

"There are two more levels," Leah said. "Let me get the espresso on. I keep the coffee maker in the darkroom."

Carl and Rosemary drifted from wall to wall, glancing at framed photographs of China and Paris and oddly-lit interiors with gaunt Asian peasants or winsome young white women. In one corner a large leather chair was stationed between shelves stacked with lush editions of photography books. A small table in front of the chair was littered with proof sheets and fashion magazines. Carl flipped through a magazine and dropped it on the table.

"This is wonderful," Rosemary said, blinking from wall to wall. "Isn't this something, Carl? I told you Leah was special."

Leah came out of the darkroom and said, "Let me show you the upstairs."

A narrow flight of stairs with no railing took them to a landing that was stacked with painted canvases.

"I'm storing these for a young painter I know in Montreal. I think I can sell them. Isn't he good?"

They stood before the paintings with thoughtful faces. Rosemary pressed a finger to her lips. Carl's first impression was that the pictures were not good, that they attempted a nearly impossible synthesis of realistic landscape and abstract design and he wanted to say as much out loud. He turned away. He realized he was still upset over being stoned by those kids.

"Yes, he's very gifted," Rosemary said. "I can see this guy's going places."

"I hate to break up the party," Carl said, "but I should hit the road."

Leah shot him a glance. She said, "But you must see the upstairs. You have to see the rest of the tower before you leave." She ushered them to the next set of stairs. "You and Rosemary go up and take a look. There's a fantastic view, really. Be very careful, and I'll turn the lights on once you've had a look."

Carl followed Rosemary up the uneven steps, groping a little until he found solid footing in the dark upper chamber. Above the fog and clouds, the moon blazed through the single tall window and he realized they were in the eye of the tower, the part that stood against the glowing sky over the river. Rosemary touched his shoulder to steady herself, then moved around in the darkness and moonlight, exclaiming softly as if Leah were there to hear her comment. Carl went to the window and looked out over the crumbling concrete and ragged bush that dissolved in the dark beyond the spotlights on that side of the building. The moon pressed the warped pane, splashing the room in phosphorescent puddles that implied ghostly humps and curves, contours that involved no common name or function. In the middle of the room Rosemary was turning and touching things, talking softly to herself, a shadow in a realm of shadows and glowing surfaces. Carl watched her and wished Leah would hit the lights. He turned back to the window and looked down on the boundary where the concrete went to weeds and scrub, and the fog-smeared halogen lamps gave way to impenetrable darkness.

"Hey," he said, moving closer to the glass. "Hey, look. What's that?"

Below him, three small figures separated from the tangled dark and emerged into the perimeter of light around the one-storey extension of the western wing. They were kids, not quite teenagers, in baseball caps and oversized lumberjack shirts. One of them moved toward the lit window of the lower building. The kid crouched and stood and drew back his arm.

"Hey!" Carl said, as if they could hear him.

For a moment the kid stood there with his arm cocked. The other two moved back without turning around. The hatless one stood farthest away, hands in pockets yet ready to run. In the posture Carl recognized him.

"Rosemary," Carl said, and the other kid let fly. From the height of the tower Carl could hear shattering glass.

"Jesus, that kid just took out a window down there!"

He tried to locate Rosemary in the dark behind him. He could hear her humming, drifting vaguely in and out of the moonlight.

"Your kid's down there, Rose. That's Talbott. They're just standing there…"

He heard another crash. When he looked the other two had vanished and the one who had thrown the rocks was running toward the dark.

The overhead lights winked on uncertainly: in a moment Leah's head and shoulders appeared at the top of the stairs.

"It's fantastic!" Rosemary said. "Just beautiful, Leah." She had taken a seat on a stack of boxes against the wall opposite the window. Her face was closed and serene.

"I thought you'd like it," Leah said. She handed a blue demitasse cup and saucer to Rosemary and started across the room with a green cup and saucer for Carl.

"Did you hear it? Those kids —"

She handed him the diminutive china and peered at him as if he'd reverted to a foreign tongue.

"Those kids just broke a window downstairs. Probably the same bunch that got my car."

Leah moved across the room and sat beside Rosemary on the boxes. Now that the lights were on Carl could see a high cluttered space, stacked with crates, strewn with winter clothes and books and antique-looking toys, all the artifacts from Leah's various lives on various continents and islands.

"Kids?" she said quietly. She folded her hands on her lap and watched Rosemary sip her coffee.

"Oh, this is lovely," Rosemary said. "This hits the spot."

"I'll get one for myself and be right back."

Carl watched her disappear down the stairs. Rosemary sighed over the hot drink and closed her eyes, as if to savour the moment.

"Do you want me to go after Talbott?" he said. "He shouldn't be running around out there. What's the time? I think I should find him."

Rosemary tasted her coffee and glanced around at the odds and ends that seemed to intrigue her.

"Rose? What do you think? Should I go down there?"

"Oh," she said, reaching into a box and lifting the sleeve of a worn cloth jacket that had once been very fashionable. "Oh, let it go, Carl. This is my first time in this place. I'll never have a first time here again. Just forget it, can't you?"

Carl stared at her. She set the cup and saucer on a box and smiled at him. This was not a place he wanted to be, he realized. The tower could have housed a gallows or a nest of vampires. He felt that nothing good would happen here.

Leah called up from the second floor: "I'm going to turn off the lights again. It's so nice to be able to see outside."

The lights went out and the moon blazed whitely through the tall window. Rosemary put her hand on Carl's thigh.

"I love it here," she said, her voice low and very near in the dark. "I'd love to fuck you here, Carl."

Leah's voice rose from the stairway as she came up again: "I knew you'd like the tower, Rosemary. This is really where I live. This is my real home."

Carl saw her shape pass in front of the moonlit window. He stood and shifted to the far wall. He listened to the women's voices moving intimately in the dark room. After a while he began to pace between the wall and the stairway.

Rosemary said, "What's wrong with you, Carl? I'm afraid Carl's got a bee in his bonnet."

He stopped and tried to focus on them in the cold white light that dappled the room. In relief against it, their figures were lithe, poised, restored to an indefinite youth. They might have been girls who had just hoisted themselves onto a dock after a summer swim.

"Sorry," he said. "I keep thinking about those kids out there."

"Don't worry," Leah said. "Your car is safe in the lot."

He tried to see her eyes in the dark. He said, "That's not it. I'm not worried about the car."

"Well, then," Rosemary told him. "Sit down and relax. Don't be a crosspatch."

"Aren't you worried about Talbott?" he asked. "Aren't you concerned about your son?"

He could see her lift her face. He thought her eyes were shut.

"I'm here with my friends now. I'm seeing things and hearing ideas I never saw or heard before. Right now, this is what I want. I can't be running after my children day in and day out. I need this."

He walked to the window and back again.

"All right," he said. "All right."

He sat on the far side of the room and listened to them talk about clothes and travel and classical dance. The talk seemed to make Rosemary smoothly expansive, as if she'd been drinking alcohol instead of caffeine, and he supposed she needed the talk, as she'd said.

Leah asked if they'd like to see her photographs and they filed down the two sets of stairs, past the paintings, to the first floor. Rosemary took the big leather chair and Carl pulled up a stool. Leah brought over another chair and placed several wide, flat boxes of prints on the small table before them. The boxes contained a hodgepodge of pictures she'd taken over the last five years. One at a time she handed them to Rosemary, who lifted her palms to take the next picture as if it were a morsel of sacrament.

"These are amazing," Rosemary said. "Just amazing," and she passed the next one to Carl. She leaned forward and absorbed each picture Leah placed in her hands. One showed a Chinese hobo smoking a pipe in a midnight train station. Another showed a radiant blonde girl in a Paris bookstore. There were many pictures of Shanghai rooftops and strings of trash floating in the Seine.

"Here's one of my favourites," Leah said. "It's one of my very few North American pictures. I took it two years ago when I was back for Christmas. We were driving home from Vermont when my son-in-law hit this deer. We're lucky it didn't come through the windshield."

Rosemary caught her breath and brought one hand to her throat. The black and white picture in her other hand showed a young doe spread against an embankment of snow-mottled earth. The long, delicate-looking legs were splayed and bent to suggest impact and recoil, the head thrown back and mouth open in an illusion of ecstasy. Looking closely, Carl saw that the eyes were beginning to occlude with death, but even then the animal had fixed on the camera with the light of a wildly desperate hope or desire.

Rosemary shook her head slowly.

"I've never seen anything like it."

Carl handed the picture back to Leah.

"Did it die?" he asked.

"Oh yes," she said, matter-of-factly. "It died while I was taking the picture."

She looked at Carl and smiled blandly. Her made-up eyes were stark ovals against her pale, dry face.

"What a story," Rosemary said. "I just can't believe the life you've had. I mean, some things have happened to me, but your life means something."

Leah smiled and dropped the pictures into the box on the table.

Carl stood and stretched his arms away from his chest. He announced that he really must go, that if either of them wanted a ride, this was it. Reluctantly, Rosemary found her coat. Leah said she'd stay and finish some work in the darkroom. She walked them out to the elevator, where Rosemary slipped her arm around Leah's waist and said, "That was beautiful. I can tell this is going to be my new home."

Leah nodded and smiled.

Later, when they parked beside her complex, Rosemary said, "At night it's almost beautiful down here. You know, being around nice things, beautiful things, does something to me."

Carl could hear the odd warmth of her voice in the dark of the car. The fog had lifted and straight ahead, down the weedy hill and beyond the cinder road, the black river reflected tiny stars.

"I was meant for such things," she said. And then, her tone narrowing, "What are we doing, Carl? Right now, what do you want to do?"

He knew she wanted him to ask for it. She wanted him to take responsibility for asking. He looked out at the river as he spoke: "You should let me come in," he said. "I think you should invite me inside."

For a moment she seemed to be staring out at whatever he was looking at. Then she said, "Come on, then."

Moving quickly, she got out of the car and clipped down the walkway in front of the townhouses. Carl caught up just as she was unlocking the front door.

The house was dark.

"Looks like nobody's here," Rosemary said.

He trailed her tentatively into the living room as she turned on a lamp. The floor and sofa were littered with rumpled clothes and coffee mugs, and a smoky taint hung in the air. Rosemary frowned and turned off the light again.

"Come on," she said. "Let's go to my room."

She moved purposefully through the dark and Carl followed the sound of her heels on the stairs.

The street lamp just outside her window shone through her room, down the hall. Rosemary drew the shade, turned on the lamp beside her bed and waited with her hand on the doorknob as Carl came in. Then she closed the door and locked it, even though the house was empty. Carl stood there while she brisked around the bed, tidying the room. She'd rearranged it again since he was here a few weeks ago.

"Do you still have your shoes on?" she said, and he realized that she'd been undressing as she put things away. He sat on the bed and pulled off his shoes. Rosemary lit two candles on the dresser, turned off the lamp, and sprawled on the bed. She didn't touch him.

"This is what you're really after, isn't it, Carl?" Her voice was both insinuating and tender. "Isn't this what you really want?"

He kissed her thigh and pressed his face against her.

"That's right," he said. "This is what I want."

"Oh yes, I know you, Carl. You say you want to help me. You want to help Rosemary. That's what you tell people. But this is what you really want, because this is all there is. Isn't that right, Carl?"

She seemed to be talking to herself now, but he answered, "That's right. You're right. This is all there is."

An hour later one of her children came home. Rosemary lay still and held a finger to her lips. They listened to noises from the kitchen, then footsteps on the stairway.

"That's Talbott," she whispered. "His sister won't come back until dawn."

She made Carl get up and push his clothes against the bottom of the door, to absorb the noise, she said.

When he lay down beside her again she was in a different

mood, musing on what had transpired that day with Leah.

"She phoned me this morning to talk about this modelling contest she knows. It's for women over thirty-five. She'll take my picture and enter two or three of the best for me. If I win I get a thousand dollars and a modelling job in the city. For a week they'll dress me and comb me and treat me like a queen."

"Great," said Carl. "But who'll stay with the kids?"

The candles were guttering out, casting snaky shadows on the ceiling.

"Oh, I'm not worried about that. Linda's old enough to look after the place."

Linda, her fifteen-year-old, had already been caught shoplifting. She was rarely at home. Talbott, who was twelve, had been to school maybe three or four times since it started two and a half months ago.

Rosemary continued: "And you know, Carl, Leah wants pictures of you and me. She wants pictures of us together."

"What do you mean, together?"

"She wants to capture the energy between us. That's what she said. She says there's some very interesting energy between us. She knows about you, Carl."

They lay there for a while with the candles flickering.

"I don't know," Carl said. "I know Leah impresses you, but I have to say I have reservations. I have to admit my enthusiasm for all this modelling and photography stuff is limited."

Rosemary made a sound of impatience. She said, "Why can't you ever be positive? Why can't you just believe in me now and then?"

He tried to choose his words. "I don't know," he said. "I'm being careful for you, I guess. I guess I know too much about you. Maybe you've told me too much about your past."

"You think I'm crazy!" she said. "You think I'm incapable of making a rational decision!"

He listened to her harsh breathing beside him, the panting noise she made when the words wouldn't come. He remembered one episode from not quite a year ago. After an evening of love-making when she had seemed tense, abrupt, not herself, she jumped up and stalked around the apartment knocking into things. Carl had rolled over to say something when he realized that he was looking at words written on her pillowcase in faded lipstick like old blood stains. The writing said: *Sex isn't love, but I love sex.* When he pointed at it, she cried, "That's right!" and she stripped off the pillowcase and threw it angrily across the room. He hadn't pursued the matter. There had been several such incidents he hadn't pursued. But they had pooled in his subconscious to form an amorphous dread, so that when she finally broke down he was neither surprised nor relieved: he understood that this was an inevitable consequence, but not yet the end. He had no sense of reaching a conclusion, or that anybody had learned anything.

"Come on, Rose. If I thought you were crazy would I be here now? Would we be having this conversation?"

"Ha," she said. "I know why you're here. Besides, you're just jealous. You're jealous of Leah."

One candle went out, and they lay in the near darkness.

"Or maybe you think I'm immoral," she said. She shifted closer to him. "That's the same as crazy to you, isn't it?"

For the sheerest instant his mind seized on the image of her face in sexual throes, the rage in her eyes, the way the marbled green-blue of her irises seemed to disintegrate with passion.

"That's what scares you and that's what you need," she said, her voice so close it seemed to enter his veins.

The other candle sputtered and went out.

She said, "You want me to keep talking to you, don't you, Carl. You need to hear this. You liar, Carl — I know you. I know you, you sweet bastard..."

Her voice was inside him, a subtle stealthy spirit inside him, talking to a part of him that was like darkness inside darkness.

"You can't fool me, Carl. You think you're protecting me, but I know why you're here."

Rosemary's voice was deep inside, and he lay there and let the voice fill up the darkness.

A week passed without Carl seeing or phoning Rosemary.
And she didn't call him. Since last summer the unspoken
understanding was that after a night together he was to leave
it alone, leave it to her to initiate the next contact. That was
how she wanted it. Once, in the middle of the week, he saw
Rosemary and Leah from across the street: they came out of a
drugstore together and set off as if pursuing important mat-
ters. Leah's arm was curled around her camera case, pressing
it to her side. Rosemary wore sunglasses Carl had never seen
before. Her hair was loose and full and seemed to advertise a
rare and uncompromising vitality. Carl stood on the sidewalk
with a box of books in his arms and watched until they disappeared around a corner.

The next day, after work, he found himself wandering
toward the river. He took the cinder road and walked slowly
past the dry docks and old warehouses where yachts and
excursion boats were repaired and hidden from the winter.
He walked on, beside the trees and the picnic tables that
straddled the water. A golden October haze had settled over
the river and in the distance he could see Leah's studio, the
reddish brick tower almost ochre in the late afternoon sun.
Around it, the waste of giant weeds stretched all the way to
the charcoal road; bits of orange and gold drifted down from
the trees and large black crows hovered and dropped from
sight below the dead branches. To his left the shabby fronts
of the townhouse apartments complicated the scene: he realized that Rosemary could look out her bedroom window and
see the lights in Leah's tower. He could imagine Rosemary
gazing across at twilight or just before she went to bed.
Likewise, Leah had a perfect view of Rosemary's place,
though he doubted she often looked in that direction.

Carl heard movement in the underbrush on the other side
of the road. A twig snapped, the weeds parted, and a long-
haired boy in a torn lumberjack shirt scampered up the bank
to the road. He fell into stride beside Carl with his hands in

his pockets, a tight, self-conscious smile on his face.

"Talbott," Carl said. "Where did you come from?"

Rosemary's son smiled and shrugged. "Down there," he said. "I know lots of places down there."

They walked along and Carl considered asking him about the rock-throwing incident. Strangely enough, Carl found it easier to like Talbott now that he was nearly a teenager. Ten months ago he'd been a loud, demanding kid. Now he was adrift in adolescence and visibly at a loss: his sister frightened him and his mother was seldom at home. Once, back in the spring before she went under, Rosemary kept Carl waiting downstairs for an hour while she laughed and talked on the phone with a former boyfriend. Carl had paced about miserably, overhearing bright fragments of chatter from the bedroom above him, until Talbott appeared with his comic book collection to show Carl. This odd gesture of kindness from a kid who'd previously had little to say made an impression on Carl. He had not forgotten it.

"So I hear you gave up on school," Carl said.

"School sucks," said the boy. "They treat me like I'm stupid. The teachers are idiots, and they make me feel like I'm the dumb one."

"Par for the course," Carl said. "It's never been any different."

A car passed them, raising a fine black powder.

"Anyhow," Carl said. "You should go to school. It beats hanging around."

"I like hanging around," Talbott said. They walked some more. Then he said, "Where are you going?"

"Me? To Leah's studio. Just over there."

Talbott nodded. "She told my mother she'd pay me by the hour if I'd let her follow me around and take pictures of me for a day. In a day I could earn enough to buy a new engine for my train. Almost."

"Maybe I could help you with that," Carl said.

He walked on, feeling the last warmth of the sun on his neck and shoulders. Far above them an airplane droned sleepily. It took him a moment to realize that Talbott had gone back. Carl stopped and turned around. He held his hand against the sky. "Hey," he said. Yards behind him, the boy waved and stepped off the road, down into the thickets of weed and broken glass.

Two youngish men were leaning against the brass rail in front of the mill entrance, across the lane from the parking lot. One of the men wore a tuxedo, the other a brown leather jacket. They both glanced at Carl and nodded as he approached. The door was open and he went inside the building. From down the hall, classical music rose faintly from someone's tape player. The elevator was waiting and he took it to the third floor. He walked past the Imagio office and looked through the glass panel on the door to Leah's studio. She was sitting in the leather chair, reading a fashion magazine. Carl tapped on the glass and she looked up. She rose quickly and came toward him with a curious, sideways movement that accentuated her hips.

"Hello. Come in. Please..." she said in her queerly subdued voice, just above a whisper. "What a surprise. How nice. Please, sit..."

She insisted that Carl take the leather chair where she'd been sitting. A shaft of fading sunshine fell on the warped hardwood floor like golden fabric and Carl felt himself ease back in the deep cushions.

"Coffee," Leah said, "we'll have coffee. I'm ready for some."

She stepped toward the darkroom and hesitated, looking at him over her shoulder. In a man's button-down shirt and black jeans and heels she looked like a busy college girl, an art student arriving late for class while the instructor winked and smiled. But her face was shrunken and shrewdly ancient.

"Here's something," she said, and she took a thick envelope from a shelf and dropped it on his lap. It was full of colour snapshots. "I took these out on the roof last week, just as the sun was going down. Of course, I won't show them to

Rosemary. They're just an experiment."

Carl looked at the pictures while she disappeared into the darkroom to put coffee on. Each photograph contained an image of Rosemary wearing a vulnerable smile and a lace shawl around bare shoulders. In each she was bathed in a sick rosy light that revealed every line and sorrow on her face. They seemed to be pictures of Rosemary grieving for Rosemary; one woman gazing sorrowfully at the other woman she had been or would be... Each shot was a variation on this pastel sadness, and in one, despite the expensive shawl, she was downright ugly, like a discount store clerk after a bad day. Carl realized that pictures could show anything about any subject. If the judges of that modelling contest saw one of these pictures they would quickly move on to the next candidate. It was a trick of the technology and light. On the other hand, her awful beauty and sadness could not be faked. They were real. It was all there, it was all Rose, depending upon the moment that caught her.

Carl returned the exposures to the envelope without a second look.

In a few minutes Leah emerged with cups and saucers, setting one pair in front of Carl on the magazine-strewn table.

"What do you think?" she said. "I won't show those to Rosemary, but they're interesting, don't you think?"

"Well," said Carl. "They're not easy to look at."

"Don't worry. I'll get some beautiful pictures of her. I'll give her some that she can use. I'm sure she'll win that contest."

Carl set the cup and saucer on the low table.

"This is hard to explain," he said, "because I'll sound like some jealous boyfriend or some kind of Puritan or something. And as you probably know, I'm not really Rosemary's boyfriend. Not really. It's hard to explain. But you must realize," he said, faltering. "It must be apparent to you that Rosemary is kind of fragile. She's not quite..." he faltered again and lifted his hands. "Oh hell, I don't know. She must have told you she was out of commission there for a few weeks. She must have told you something about herself on that count."

Leah blinked at him. "You mustn't worry," she said quietly. "I would never do anything to hurt Rosemary."

"No, but... Well, this fashion gambit. And all this emphasis on her looks. This isn't the first time people have taken pictures of her." He drew a heavy breath. "And it's never turned out well. Her last husband, the bad one... He took movies of her and sold them to his friends. You know. It was a real violation. It really screwed her up."

Leah placed the small blue cup and saucer on the table beside his and picked up the photographs.

"She's such a lovely girl," she said, flipping through the snapshots. "I know she'll win that contest."

Carl pushed forward in the leather seat.

"What I'm trying to say is, I don't think the contest or modelling will be good for Rose. I know it's presumptuous of me to speak like this, but I know her pretty well. I know her story. Her luck is bad. Even when it's good it's bad. If she wins it'll be like a trapdoor opening under her. Giving herself to the camera does something to her. I've seen it. It's not healthy."

Leah stood and took a deluxe edition of somebody's photographs from the bookshelf. She scowled slightly at the cover.

"At first she tried to play sexy for me," Leah said. "She tried to play sexy, but I wouldn't let her do it. That's not what I wanted."

Carl spoke slowly: "She doesn't have the radar the rest of us have that warns us away from the bad stuff. She doesn't have it. She falls for all the wrong things and people. It probably isn't even safe for her to have her picture published."

Leah sighed. "She's a beautiful girl. Such a beautiful girl."

"She's a forty-three-year-old woman with two very troubled kids."

Leah slid the oversized book back onto the shelf. She said, "Rosemary is exactly what they're looking for. I just know she can win that contest and get some work."

Carl felt the blind insistence behind Leah's mild and pliant voice. It seemed to encircle his logic with tendrils of wilfulness.

"You know," she said, "I can tell you love Rosemary very much. But I can't see you in her future. Maybe I shouldn't say it. But I can't see you with her far down the road."

He stared at the mellow light in the window. He knew that others probably told Rosemary the same. He knew that if Leah said as much to her she would believe it. She'd believe what Leah said over the evidence at hand, all the favours and attention Carl had bestowed throughout the summer.

He stood slowly and snugged the zipper of his jacket.

"I should be going," he said.

Leah blinked at him several times. "Oh, wait," she said. "Don't go yet. I had something to ask you. I wanted your opinion."

He waited.

"You see, I need to make up some business cards, but I'm not sure which image to use. Here, let me show you."

She went into the darkroom again and quickly reappeared with a couple of postcard-sized photographs she thrust into Carl's hand.

He stood beside the fuzzy rectangle of light from the large window and studied the pictures. The first showed a camera on a tripod and a woman behind it focusing, so her face was hidden. She wore only a man's floppy shirt, unbuttoned as she stooped, flowing open to reveal the perfect globe of one breast. The other picture featured the same woman, this time totally naked save for a derby hat which she dipped forward to obscure the top half of her face. The other hand was on her hip, which was shapely and firm, and her breasts fell slightly forward in a manner that revealed their roundness and weight. The pose with the hat was not original. Carl felt certain he'd seen it somewhere before, though he couldn't say where.

He looked from one picture to the other several times. Leah leaned close, a little behind him. Then he understood that this was Leah in the pictures. Behind the camera and the hat. Her flesh was white and smooth, surprisingly youthful in both cases below her hidden face.

"When were these taken?" he asked.

"Last summer, when I was setting up the studio. I thought I might use one for a business card — you know, photographers make up postcards from their work and mail them out to advertise. I thought one of these might make a stir in this town."

Carl nodded. He looked at the pictures again and passed them back to her.

"Very interesting," he said. "Thanks for showing them to me."

She clasped the photographs in her hands, which might have been the hands of a ninety-year-old Chinese woman she had photographed.

"I should go," he said, and he moved toward the door.

"Wait. Why don't you stay a while? Sit and read a book while I finish in the darkroom. I have some beautiful books you could look at, books that are quite rare, actually."

"Really, I should go," he said.

She stared at him and clapped her hands together lightly.

"Do you know," she said, "it's Friday the 13th! Something wonderful always happens to me on Friday the 13th. Something special always happens."

Somehow this news dismayed him.

"Oh!" she said softly, pressing closer, "the way you're leaning on the door frame is something I'd love to photograph. I'd love to get a picture of that gesture."

He straightened and waved at her.

"Well, good luck with your work. I guess we'll see you soon."

She followed him into the corridor, down to the elevator.

The doors opened and began to close.

"Wait!" she said.

He hit the button and they opened again: Leah skipped into the elevator and kissed him on the lips. He saw the heavily outlined ovals of her eyes come up to his. Her mouth was dry like parchment, like pressed flowers. Then she drew back and the doors shut. On the way down he vowed he would never show up in Leah's darkroom. Whatever happened, he would not let himself be photographed.

That Saturday night, while Carl was doing dishes, the telephone rang. He snatched it up and flung the dish towel over his shoulder.

"Hello, Carl," Rosemary said in a mysterious, aristocratic tone. "What are you doing right now?"

He could hear public sounds behind her and for a second he thought she was calling from work. But she never worked Saturday nights. Before he could answer, she said, "Leah and I are at the Emerson Grill, and we want you to come down and buy us a bottle of wine." The Grill was the place they'd gone to celebrate that first night back in the summer. "Oh come on, Carl. Drive down and we'll have a little party. Leah specifically asked me to ask you."

"All right," he said. "I can do that. I wasn't doing anything anyhow."

"Well hurry," she said and she broke the connection.

Carl changed and drove toward downtown. He tuned in a station from New York City that his car radio picked up only at night, a station that played popular standards from the '30s, '40s and '50s — big band and show tunes and torch songs. One Sunday night, just before Rosemary disappeared for those several months, they'd parked the car beside the river and listened to a poignantly surreal version of "Me and My Shadow." Carl envisioned the male crooner wearing tails and a top hat and a black Mardi Gras mask, out among the stars playing the constellations as if they were magical vibes, tapping each star with a mallet that produced a clear silvery tone. Rosemary had started to cry, because the music was so sweet and strange she said, because she remembered her mother and brothers back in England singing this very song. But Carl had sensed something else. Something coming. From the start with Rosemary he'd been able to name her particular troubles, identify their sources and predict an outcome, even before she'd admitted them to herself. He'd taken no pride or pleasure in this ability, but so far he hadn't mustered the will to break the wavelength.

As soon as Carl stepped into the restaurant he heard her voice carrying above the general din of the crowd. He walked toward the table where she was ensconced with Leah and three men he'd never seen before. Rosemary was sheathed in a tight purple minidress and several silk scarves: her legs stretched away from the table, posed at a provocative angle, her stockings reflecting the sheen of an ideal light.

"Here's Carl," she cried, sitting up a little. "This is the guy we were telling you about."

The men glanced at him as if they were comparing his actual image to what Rosemary had conveyed. Slightly out of the action, her chair to one side, Leah sat holding a wine glass, smiling her prescient oriental smile.

"Now don't kill the party, Carl," Rosemary declared. "I told them you were awfully righteous and likely to say something damp."

He took off his jacket and looked around for a seat.

"Sounds like you've had a few," he said.

"See! What did I tell you?" she said. "Yes, as a matter of fact, we're all a little squiffy. What of it? Who cares?"

Rosemary had no tolerance for alcohol: one glass of wine made her silly, two made her manic and liable to say anything. She'd once told him about how she'd gotten drunk at a New Year's Eve party and found herself involved in a threeway with a man and his half-sister. The story had bewildered Carl, mostly because he'd never been able to determine whether or not she'd known what she was doing while she did it. She herself wasn't quite able to answer that one.

"Hello, Carl," Leah said, scooting her chair. "Where would you like to sit?"

He slid a seat between Rosemary and a man with silver sideburns in a silver-grey double-breasted suit. The man kept his eyes on something in the middle of the table as Carl pushed in beside him.

"Very pretty," said the man across the table. "Very, very

striking indeed."

Leah said, "They'll look better printed up on fibre. That's just cheap resin-coated paper."

Carl realized they were looking at Leah's proof-sheets, multiple black-and-white images of Rosemary in various poses, in various clothes. The men were solid business types, physically solid with slabby limbs and barrel bodies packed into pin-striped suits. There was a mentholated quality to them which seemed to emanate from a general lacquer over their hair and hands and suits. Carl couldn't tell if they were more interested in the pictures or the original who chattered at them as they passed the proof-sheets back and forth. Somehow the pictures seemed to validate the real woman, to show her in a trophy light the men could appreciate with their solid business sense.

"We got tired of waiting for you, Carl," Rosemary said, oddly shining in their attention. She did not introduce the men. She said, "We got tired of waiting, and these guys drove up in two different Jaguars. We saw them through the window. We just knew they were from out of town and needing company."

"You're half right anyhow," said the man with the sideburns. "So happens we're all just hometown folks."

Rosemary laughed. Somebody had put a straight scotch in front of her and she was taking it in hungry little sips.

"Hard to believe," said the third man. He lit a cigarette, which was also pin-striped, and tapped it over the glass dish. He raised a finger toward Rosemary and said, "Where did you come from?"

She laughed again and scattered breathless, disparate fragments about herself in stories that had no beginning or end. The men nodded and glanced from Rosemary to the pictures in their hands. Carl saw the images like a disjointed movie of Rosemary framed in their thick, pale fingers, the glint of their heavy rings like bright side ornaments. But he was determined to stick it out. For Rosemary's sake, he would not leave. Not yet.

She swivelled and lifted her legs above the table like a show girl. For an instant they glittered in the dim turquoise light. Then she lowered them to Carl's lap, her ankles crossed just above his thigh. She talked at the men in non sequiturs and giddy asides, her remarks like little pink flags pasted to the obscured and omitted information they really wanted. They were intrigued and baffled by Rosemary and her talk, like duck hunters confronted suddenly with flamingos. With slitted eyes they sighted her down their drinks and through the smoke.

One of them said, "Looking at these photos I'd have a hard time guessing your age."

Rosemary beamed at him. "Leah's a brilliant artist. She's going to make me famous. Or at least rich. We're going to enter these pictures in a nationwide contest and split the winnings."

"You'll win, all right," said the man with sideburns. "No doubt about it in my mind."

"Leah's done modelling herself. She came along at just the right moment. Isn't she beautiful? Aren't we just the pair? Oh, she has the most stunning pearls!"

Leah smiled neutrally, as if she were meditating in thin, Tibetan air. For an instant the men regarded her, then they turned their attention back to Rosemary.

"When I saw these photographs," she said, "I knew my life had changed. All my life people have been telling me to go for it, that I could sell myself in pictures. It was like a drink they kept offering. They kept saying, 'Here, Rosemary, drink this. You'll like it.' And I kept pushing it aside. Well, now I'm ready. And I think I'll like it. I like it already!"

"Hear, hear," said one of the men, raising his glass.

She made a funny warbling sound and shook her hair over her eyes. One of the men applauded, as if she were about to honour him with a song. Carl looked around hopelessly. This had been a favourite place for them — the place Carl and

Rosemary went to make up, to celebrate, to find that mutual wavelength. Here it was possible to imagine they were in a different town, a different climate, and thus transcend the shabby stuff that jammed communication. Tonight there was a larger-than-usual Saturday night crowd, slightly upscale, with martini glasses and exotic appetizers. On another Saturday night he would have been in his element, wholly at ease.

A familiar song came down from the sound system. Rosemary swung her feet to the floor and began to shimmy in her chair.

"I love this song!" she said. "Oh, I love dancing to this one!"

"Would you like to?" said the man with the sideburns.

"I don't think there's dancing here," Rosemary said. "I don't think they'd let us."

The man shrugged. "So what are they going to do? Throw us out? I don't think so. I think you could do just about anything you wanted to here."

Rosemary coloured with girlish delight. "Why thank you, kind sir," she said theatrically, tipsily. "Well, why not then? All right. You're on, buster. Let's do it."

They stood, joined hands, and moved to a clear spot in the middle of the room. Heads turned. They began to do a slow, cool twist to the music. Somebody whistled and applauded. A few diners shifted their chairs to make space. The waitresses stared, partly annoyed, partly entertained.

Carl lifted somebody else's drink and put it down.

It was that word "buster" that had broken his resolve.

One of the men leaned toward Leah. "Let me ask you something about your friend..."

Carl listened to their lowered voices for a minute, then he rose and steered around the dancing couple toward the door.

The phone rang seconds after he arrived home. He frowned at the instrument on the wall, then lifted the receiver. At first he did not recognize Leah's voice. It was unusually forceful and clear.

"I wanted to see if you went away upset tonight," she said.

"You seemed upset."

He stood in the dark of his kitchen and listened. He could hear no background noise. Her voice came fast and high.

"I didn't know those guys at the table," she said. "Rosemary invited them to join us. She's so spontaneous, so free."

"Very free," Carl said. He thought Leah sounded younger, no longer the voice of the female Judas tree. He laughed out loud. He had the urge to use that phrase over the phone.

"Well, they were sort of sleazy," Leah said lightly, mistaking his laughter. "And you're right about Rosemary. She's not quite an adult sometimes. She lacks discretion. I don't know why she said that about my pearls. She's never seen my pearls. I mentioned them to her, but she's never seen them. And I really don't like the fact that I own them broadcast to strangers."

Carl's spell of humour suddenly vanished. He bore down on the receiver in his hand.

"Time for me to go," he said. "She's your case now."

"Carl," Leah said. "Listen to me. I'm a loner. I've always been a loner. Rosemary is a lovely, lovely woman, but she knows that I can't be responsible for her."

"Does she? You better make sure of that. If you send those pictures for her, she'll win," and just then, saying it, he knew that it was true. She'd won already. She was fated.

"It will be a tremendous opportunity for her."

"Maybe," Carl said. He stood in the dark, waiting.

"Carl, listen. Listen, Carl. I'm going to Paris over the holidays. Have you seen Paris? You should come along. I know a perfect little hotel on the Left Bank, very economical if the proprietors like you. You'd love it. It would be good for you to get away from here for a while."

Carl listened to the strange girlish voice that came over the wire, the voice he had not heard before. While it talked he realized that he had spent months, summer and fall, trying to bring Rosemary back, bring her back to himself, his friends, bring her back to the land of the living. He had honestly believed in that place and that he could take her there. And he'd almost done it. For a month or so, she had been with him again, almost like before. They had gotten to the threshold, they were waiting for the door to open, when Leah appeared. But it was all too much and he was so tired. Tired to the core. And he hated the telephone. God, how he hated the telephone.

"Leah," he said. "I don't like you. Okay? I don't like what you do on this earth. I can't name it. I can't nail you on this one. But I want you to know that I see it, I comprehend, and I really don't like it. I know you take good pictures, but I really hate what you do. All right? Okay? So please leave me alone now. Just stay away."

The silence on the other end was vivid. He thought that she was shocked. He listened hard. In a moment the dial tone droned in his ear. He hadn't heard the cut-off and it was possible that she'd hung up even before he'd told her to stay away.

Just after noon the next day Carl was sitting at the desk in the back of Allen's bookstore. Allen was out getting coffee and the store was empty but for one old man hidden behind the religion section. Now and then the man cleared his throat as though he were about to make an announcement. A leaden grey light fell through the big window in the storefront; Carl watched pedestrians cross paths on the sidewalk, their heads down, their pace brisk, engaged in necessary but routine errands. When Allen returned Carl said he needed a break and Allen told him to go ahead.

On the street he fell in with passers-by and followed the stream to the end of the block. At the light he felt a vibration from the shifting grey skies; he lifted his head and decided that the season's first snow was imminent. Across the street, Mitch and Stan were walking in the other direction. Mitch carried his oversized camera in one hand like a lunker salmon or lake trout, hefting it with reserved masculine pride. Likewise, Stan bore his oboe case on his back, slung there with a colourful peasant rig of red and green cords. He was talking happily to the stoic Mitch and leaning forward a little under his instrument, pushing the curly black hair away from his face with a Puckish two-handed gesture. In one way, the shapely implements they bore represented soundness and vocation, identity in the world: Carl could see that Rosemary was only seeking the same. In exploiting her own image she was looking for a ready answer to strangers and citizens when they asked her what she did in the world. He heard Stan's laughter blend with the sound of traffic flowing through the intersection.

Carl walked down another block and turned north, passed the court buildings and then across a wide parking lot to the cinder road that led to Rosemary's house and Leah's studio. Rain had fallen most of the previous night and the road had turned to half-frozen black paste and potholes scummed with partial ice. He walked by the weathered boat-houses and along the scruffy park: the trees were bare and the river to his right was cold to look at. The road stretched toward the low-rent townhouses and the distant mill. Carl walked a little farther and sat at one of the picnic tables. He could clearly make out Rosemary's place up ahead to the left. He wondered why he had tried so hard, after all. Why had he tried to show her the desperation he'd seen in the idea of selling herself on film? Had he feared that she'd recognize that desperation sooner or later in her own literal image, that the fact of her age and mortality would overwhelm her? Or had he just been trying to save her for himself. The endeavour at bringing her back, he understood, had been fraught with bad psychology from the start, from that summer night she'd reappeared at his patio table. He knew why he had believed that she need-ed his friends and the safety of their world, but what mattered was what Rosemary thought, what she wanted — and on that count he was still confused. Still, he couldn't escape the feel-ing that he had failed her. They all had. Now she was gone.

He gazed at the sky over the mill, the way it seemed to push darkly against the red brick tower from behind. Between him and the mill the tangled waste of scrub trees and stumps and splintery brown weeds lay like a no man's land where awful battles had been fought long ago. He seemed to be looking at the physical effects of some higher combat, some plane where logic fought impulse, where love collided with the Way Of The World in a battle that was as ultimate as it was irrelevant.

As Carl sat there he noticed someone moving down the slope from the housing units. In a moment he recognized Talbott in a worn overcoat, bareheaded, hunching across the frozen cinders. His pale face was fixed on something ahead in the underbrush, in the sere weeds that stood like spears and jagged teeth. The boy waded into the field, veered away from the river and stopped beside some larger, fallen trees. For long seconds he stood there, as though trying to decide something. Then, slowly, he hunkered down among the bare branches and the dead grass and squatted near the base of a toppled trunk. Carl could just make out the faded green of his coat, motionless among the limbs that were like the exposed rib cage of some mammoth beast. Carl waited, but the boy did not move. And while Carl sat there, watching, a particular white snow sifted down from the darkening sky, slowly falling over the brown landscape and the icy black road. Each particle seemed to make a small noise, a distinct tick on the dead leaves and frozen grass. A thin, shifting curtain of snow stretched across the pewter surface of the river and blurred the fronts of the townhouses. Carl could barely see the green coat in the underbrush below the down-curved branches. Snow gathered on the coat, but the boy did not move. The snow fell thicker and soon there was only the mottled fallen tree where the coat had been. Farther on, the tower had become a shadow, like the smudge left by something that had hung on a bleached wall. Carl brushed the snowflakes from his eyelashes to stare at the dead, whitening world. Then he stood and started back to town.

Other titles from Insomniac Press:

Dying for Veronica
by Matthew Remski

A love story of bizarre proportions, Matthew Remski's first novel is set in Toronto. Dying for Veronica is a gritty and mysterious book, narrated by a man haunted by a twisted and unhappy childhood and obsessed with the sister he loves. This shadowy past explodes into an even more psychologically disturbing present — an irresistible quest and a longing that cannot be denied. Remski's prose is beautiful, provocative, poetic: rich with the dark secrets and intricacies of Catholic mythology as it collides with, and is subsumed by, North American culture.

5 1/4" x 8 1/4" • 224 pages • trade paperback with flaps
1-895837-40-5 • $18.99

Carnival: a Scream In High Park reader
edited by Peter McPhee

One evening each July an open-air literary festival is held in Toronto's High Park. It is a midway of diverse voices joined in celebration of poetry and story telling. Audiences exceeding 1,200 people gather under the oak trees to hear both well known and emerging writers from across the country, such as, Lynn Crosbie, Claire Harris, Steven Heighton, Nicole Brossard, Nino Ricci, Al Purdy, Susan Musgrave, Leon Rooke, Christopher Dewdney, Barbara Gowdy, bill bissett... This book collects the work (much of it new and previously unpublished) from the 48 writers who have performed at Scream in High Park in its first three years.

5 1/4" x 8 1/4" • 216 pages • trade paperback with flaps
1-895837-38-3 • $18.99

Beneath the Beauty
by Phlip Arima

Beneath the Beauty is Phlip Arima's first collection of poetry. His work is gritty and rhythmic, passionate and uncompromising.

His writing reveals themes like love, life on the street and addiction. Arima has a terrifying clarity of vision in his portrayal of contemporary life. Despite the cruelties inflicted and endured by his characters, he is able to find a compassionate element even in the bleakest of circumstances.

Arima has a similar aesthetic to Charles Bukowski, but there is a sense of hope and dark romanticism throughout his work. Phlip Arima is a powerful poet and storyteller, and his writing is not for the faint of heart.

5 1/4" x 8 1/4" • 80 pages • trade paperback
isbn 1-895837-36-7 • $11.99

What Passes for Love
by Stan Rogal
   What Passes for Love is a collection of short stories which shows the dynamics of male-female relationships. These ten short stories by Stan Rogal resonate with many aspects of the mating rituals of men and women: paranoia, obsession, voyeurism, and assimilation.
   Stan Rogal's first collection of stories, *What Passes for Love*, is an intriguing search through many relationships, and the emotional turmoil within them. Stan's writing reflects the honesty and unsentimentality, previously seen in his two books of poetry and published stories. Throughout *What Passes for Love* are paintings by Kirsten Johnson.
   5 1/4" x 8 1/4" • 144 pages • trade paperback
   isbn 1-895837-34-0 • $14.99

Bootlegging Apples on the Road to Redemption
by Mary Elizabeth Grace
   This is Grace's first collection of poetry. It is an exploration of the collective self, about all of us trying to find peace; this is a collection of poetry about searching for the truth of one's story and how it is never heard or told, only experienced. It is the second story: our attempts with words to express the sounds and images of the soul. Her writing is soulful, intricate and lyrical. The book comes with a companion CD of music/poetry compositions which are included in the book.
   5 1/4" x 8 1/4" • 80 pages • trade paperback with cd
   isbn 1-895837-30-8 • $21.99

The Last Word: an insomniac anthology of canadian poetry
edited by michael holmes
   The Last Word is a snapshot of the next generation of Canadian poets, the poets who will be taught in schools — voices reflecting the '90s and a new type of writing sensibility. The anthology brings together 51 poets from across Canada, reaching into different regional, ethnic, sexual and social groups. This varied and volatile collection pushes the notion of an anthology to its limits, like a startling Polaroid. Proceeds from the sale of *The Last Word* will go to Frontier College, in support of literacy programs across Canada.
   5 1/4" x 8 1/4" • 168 pages • trade paperback
   isbn 1-895837-32-4 • $16.99

Insomniac Press • 378 Delaware Ave.
Toronto, Ontario, Canada • M6H 2T8
phone: (416) 536-4308 • fax: (416) 588-4198
email: insomna@pathcom.com